TABLE OF CONTENTS

This book is dedicated to the great writer and social philosopher Kurt Vonnegut, Jr., 1923-2007.

KILGORE TROUT
"And so it goes."

AUTHOR'S NOTE

I wish to thank and acknowledge the help of the following folks who made this book even remotely possible:

My editor for this book was Kathy Hernandez of MurderOne Inc. ("Killer Research, Writing, Editing and Proofreading"). She managed to wade through this manuscript and make sense of it all. A lot of her talent is in this book as well. But like any good editor, one hardly notices any intrusion...

To Jeorgie Winsberg of DeSoto Productions in Albuquerque, New Mexico who cleaned up a real mess of a cover in a Jumping Jack Flash moment...

My parents and family, who know how I can be about my scribbling. It just runs in the family, folks...

All the modern technology in the 21st Century -- when it works...

To Amazon.com, who catapulted this book out into the Great Wide Cyber-Yonder...

To the crooks at BookTango.com, who showed how venial and lousy the independent book publishing world can be...

And most of all I wish to thank *you* the reader for taking your time in reading this Texas Tall Tale...

Gerald Allen Loeb
May 21, 2018

When asked later in life his one regret, "Wahoo Dan" Deacon had a quick answer: "My nickname."

As it turned out he was about right. In the spring of 1926, Emily and Roger Deacon settled in what they thought was a perfect spot to raise their soon-to-be born son – Wahoo, Texas.

Now, Wahoo wasn't exactly a thriving place then. In fact, there were less than 300 souls who lived within a ten-mile radius of the place and dust lay every where. The reddish and orange-gray dirt permeated everything in the northwest plains of Texas, just a stone's throw (with a car) from New Mexico.

Wahoo was the kind of place a traveler would pass around rather than through. After all, the great national highway was a generation and a half away. But Wahoo had one valuable commodity that kept the town alive –the dirt and its cousin, clay. The clay was smelted and used for plates, ceramic molds but most notably cheap bricks that were later painted red.

After the bricks were completed in the smelter at the east edge of town, they were transported by railway to Denver, where the bricks bearing the stamp of "Wahoo – #1190" on their left side were sent to all parts east, west, north and south. The plant employed 141 of the denizens of Wahoo and was naturally its biggest employer.

The plant owner, Regis Green, was an amiable gentleman in his mid-fifties who took his civic responsibilities seriously, since he was also the mayor, chief of police and fire marshal. He also paid more taxes than anyone else so he felt entitled to be in charge.

He also owned almost as much land as his problematic neighbor Frank Manstill, who was a old-school, conservative rancher. In fact, he didn't even own a car even though his wealth almost rivaled Green's. When the Deacons arrived that spring, a small power struggle in the little town was starting to emerge. Had they known that fact, they may not have moved to the small bucolic

1

town perched at the edge of the West Texas Plains.

Roger and Emily Deacon were childhood sweethearts from Oak Park, Illinois. Roger was a brawny bear of a man, six feet and one inch tall with large, prominent upper arms. At twenty-three, he also filled out his clothes with a weight of 220 pounds, not all of it fat. His hair was black and bushy and cut a little long in the back, which was popular at the time.

He believed in using his head as well as his muscles and would probably be the most literate brick maker at the Wahoo Brick Factory. He even went to college for two years in 1923 and 1924 but had to leave when his father died, leaving his mother and two sisters alone. Nevertheless, he went to work to support them and did not regret it.

Emily was also large, for a woman. She was five feet, ten inches tall and hefty, probably 180 pounds or more. Her auburn hair was usually tied in a knot or when she lay with Roger, fanned out sensuously on their bed. She also had a mean temper sometimes that meant trouble for him. But, she had a strong loving side so that made it fine because Roger worshipped her, temper and all.

It was her eyes that attracted Roger at first — cat-like and all-knowing, Emily's "windows to the world" were green and strikingly glowing, or at least he thought so. He was 14 when he met her and immediately fell in love.

After nine years together, they were finally husband and wife.

When she announced that she was pregnant, Roger was overjoyed. When her mood swings worsened, he wasn't so sure. During her early pregnancy, Emily could be seen strolled in the street in Oak Park shaking her fists at other women who glared with disapproving looks because she was obviously *enceinte* – pregnant - in public, no less. They were a not yet a married couple and that further provoked the convicting stares of the offended women who lived in the fashionable suburb.

They married just when Emily could no longer hide her generous belly. Two days after their nuptials, they boarded a train from

Chicago and rode a thousand miles to Wahoo. The couple moved into a modest two-room, one bath, mud-red brick house just six blocks away from the ancient Wahoo Brick Factory. Emily constantly complained about the dust and dirt from the swirling Texas winds and the smell upwind.

She was right about the dirt – it got into everything: their clothes, the nooks and crannies in the house and even inside sealed jars. The town's biggest claim to fame was also choking it to death, slowly but surely.

So when Hamilton Daniels was found murdered in the brick quarry, even the ever-present dirt and dust was overlooked in the tumult.

*****

CHAPTER ONE:
BROWN DIRT AND BRICKS

"This looks like a decent place," Roger Deacon remarked after a quick look around. "We'll like it here."

Wahoo, Texas was a tiny West Texas town. On this April day, fifteen stone and wooden buildings were arranged in a north-south pattern with eight side streets. Most of the buildings were two and three story affairs. On the dusty main street, horses and slightly beat-up black Ford Model-Ts were parked next to each other. Orange-grey dirt was scattered everywhere on the walkways and even the rooftops. It was the first thing Roger noticed as he and his wife Emily rode into town on the Southern Pacific Western Traveler railway.

After their bags were taken off the train, a chagrined Emily Deacon surveyed the surroundings, too. "You have got to be kidding," she bitingly answered. She also noticed the dust and dirt. It was very hot and Emily wanted a bath in the worst way after their two thousand-or-more-mile train trip and the third-class accommodations that were not the best. "Why is it here of all places?"

"We've been over that before," Roger answered with the voice of a man tired of discussed this topic to death before leaving Illinois and on the train journey -- or so he thought. "Because there are jobs here in Texas, Emily. You'll see."

Roger was right. The biggest employer was the Wahoo Brick Company, who employed 99 people in the town of 307, or at least that's what the town's chalk-updated, brown-withered sign said a mile outside of town on Old Highway 134.

In Roger's pocket was a letter from the plant owner Regis Green with an offer of a job as Deputy Factory Foreman; he was very determined to make a new start with Emily here. After all, the town and much of the American West were founded by people who wanted a new start and Roger and Emily were no exception.

As for the town's name, well – that's another story.

The town was founded by the young Thomas Wahoo, who established a small town and farm nearby in 1839 as part of a land grant he inherited from his father, Abraham, a farmer from Tennessee.

Abraham had moved to Texas after his wife, Loretta and one-year-old daughter, Kathy, died of cholera in the winter of 1819. Only Thomas, his seven-year-old son, was left. Heartsick after his family was devastated, Abraham applied for a land grant from the Mexican government and he received a reply and a positive offer only two months later.

With the young boy in tow, he took Thomas, left Tennessee and never looked back and settled in Texas. He prospered as a cattle rancher and potato farmer, tilling his acreage with the fury of a man possessed. He never did remarry.

Abraham was content to let the local Mexican officials get their taxes and occasional side of free beef. He shared an occasional tequila with the Mexican tax agents and largely work peaceably under the otherwise lax Mexican administration. This relative peace was broken, however, when hostilities broke out between the Texans and Mexican President Santa Ana.

When he was urged by his rancher friends to join in the growing movement against Mexico, Abraham replied, "Why? They have always been okay with me." But his personal alliance changed after the famous battle at the Alamo in March. He became an ardent Texas freedom fighter who stayed and plowed the fields even harder.

Two days after the Massacre at Goliad where Santa Ana ordered 600 Texas rebels murdered in cold blood, a massive shipment of 89,000 pounds of corn, apples and potatoes and a herd of 300 cattle migrated from Abraham's farm to Sam Houston's forces on the Brazos River. The trip was dangerous and took almost two weeks, but young Thomas, Abraham and seven loyal ranch hands maneuvered between the Mexican Army and the flat-lands to deliver the much-needed food and supplies to the rebels.

Abraham was there in April when Sam Houston cornered Santa Ana and his sleeping Army at San Jacinto and routed then in an hour, thus ending the Texas War of Independence, as the Texans called it for years.

As a Texas patriot, Abraham personally funded every cent of the journey. It paid for almost exhausted his entire small fortune of $2,867, but is also ensured that Thomas would stay and help him with the farm and not wind up dead against the Mexicans, at least in a direct fight.

After the war, Abraham was recognized for his contribution and was allowed to keep the land he already owned under the former Mexican land grant. The New Republic of Texas threw in another 500 acres as a token of their appreciation. The new government also offered to pay him back for his contribution to the cause, but the proud rancher would have nothing of it.

"It was the right thing to do," Abraham said when asked why he almost bankrupted himself for a cause.

Before Abraham died three years later, he willed the 710-acre cattle farm to Thomas, now 27 years old. The other 120 acres he bequeathed the surviving six Mexican *vaqueros* who braved certain death in helping him had they been caught by the Mexican Army. A descendant of one of those men, Javier Hermosa Arreno, later became the first Mexican elected to the Texas State Legislature as a representative in 1974.

Thomas eagerly tackled the many obligations and problems of a large farm and worked hard to increase his personal property, even establishing a town in the land called the New Texas Republic.

When government officials asked him what to name it, Thomas thought and said, "Wahoo Valley." Thomas always said there was

6

no particular reason for the name. He just liked the sound of it.

Unfortunately, the clerk who recorded the new name at the one-story stucco statehouse in now-Austin, Texas, carelessly omitted the word "Valley" on the official documents and no one caught the error. Two months later a rider approached the farm and handed Thomas an official letter naming him "Township Administrator" of "Wahoo, Texas, until further notice."

Thomas married, had seven children and worked hard to largely help populate the fledgling town. He sent a flurry of newsletters and letters to editors of many Eastern newspapers encouraging people to come and build homesteads on this semi-barren land. He was a Texas version of P.T. Barnum without the fraud and hype.

He continued working until his death in 1890 at the age of 78. The rotund, happy man earned respect from almost everyone in town was always quick to note his biggest achievements: finding "this jewel" with his father and pushing for a railroad line in 1882 to connect the town to others.

In 1885, someone noticed that the thick dirt and clay that blanketed almost everything had particular molding properties and made an amazingly strong brick when baked under a fiery kiln. Within the year, the Wahoo Brick Factory was founded by the elder Regis Green, Jr. from Portsmouth, New Hampshire.

Wahoo grew pretty quickly after that. The area's bricks were highly prized throughout the country for their toughness and durability; in fact, these very bricks drawn from this soil and the imposing quarry north of the town square and fired in the four-story factory a mile away were used to largely rebuild San Francisco after the 'quake in 1906. It was an irony that was not lost on Roger Deacon, as Emily's parents were killed in that very same disaster.

As far as Roger was concerned, it was just fine with him to come here and start over. He and Emily had family problems from which they were trying to escape. Emily had a cantankerous but rich old uncle, Lester Hopewell Taylor. The old man had taken

Emily in as a six-year-old child after her parents were killed and she ultimately became his caretaker.

Roger knew that here in Wahoo, Uncle Lester could no longer exert any influence over their lives. He had bitterly opposed their marriage in the first place. As far as Roger was concerned, he could sit in his large Victorian mansion and brood alone with his fortune of gold, bonds, securities, silver and cash. Lester never did trust banks with his money, so he liberally sprinkled his booty throughout his nine-room home, and managed to secrete almost $2 million in various boxes, contraptions and hidden panels.

Emily tapped one of his "forgotten mother lodes" for $6,000 in cash and a set of silver gold coins before she left the surly bastard a year earlier to be with Roger. So far, the police hadn't come looking for her, so he hadn't noticed yet. Roger certainly didn't know, either. He would have been appalled by his new wife's actions. Now the cash and silver were sitting comfortably in Emily's valise, waiting to help her start a new life.

Instinctively Emily knew it was wrong to steal his money, but she also felt she had something coming to her after years of enduring his verbal abuse and nursing his injuries from falling off dead drunk off his horses (and twice from his car). Besides, she reasoned, he'll never notice the missing money -- the eccentric coot had no idea how much money he had in that house, anyway.

She had a plan: come back to Oak Park after Lester died, take a crowbar to his house and become really rich. It was a dream she first had at fifteen and was expected to care for Lester. Almost a dozen years later, she still waited for Lester to die. But one day she would come back – and then she would show those snotty hussies then! The very thought of this fantasy always made her smile slightly crookedly. It created a cold glint in her eye, no matter where she was or what she was doing at the time.

She would humor Roger for now and come to this dusty Texas town that didn't even have streetlights, a real main street or even a music hall. Emily was still biding her time and Wahoo was as good a place as any to do it. Plus, now there was the baby to consider. Emily was almost eight months pregnant when they did arrive in Wahoo although she hid it well.

The company offered Roger and Emily a small red-brick house on the edge of Waterbury Street located only a quarter mile from the Brick Factory for the fair price of $47 a month. For his labor, Roger would make a very nice $250 a month wage working in the belching, busy factory. For the first week, Emily battled the dust, dirt and her own bodily changes. She completely cleaned the two-bedroom, one-story house while Roger went to work in his new job of learning brick-making, Wahoo style.

This nice idyll would not last long.

*****

Roger Deacon sat with his back to the wall in the lower part of the factory in his office. His new boss, Jack Welborn, the plant manager, dumped a bunch of paperwork on Roger's desk less than an hour before quitting time. Scattered there were orders, dispatches, and train schedules. Although his office was below ground level, the constant heat from the nearby giant kiln made it feel like a boiler-room gone crazy.

He stared out the door and thought about what he had seen two days before. Roger had taken a car to the quarry a mile away to deliver a new drill bit for Old Marse, the factory's oldest drill. After he delivered the part and oversaw its inspection, he personally tested it before turning the machine over to the operator.

Roger's bladder was about to burst, so he walked off to some Mesquite bushes to relieve himself when he saw the splintered body of Hamilton Daniels sprawled in the dirt. Shocked, he forgot about his own bodily needs and ran to the quarry foreman's office.

"Jack, Jack!" Roger yelled as he ran into Jack Welborn's rabbit warren of an office. "Call Regis Green immediately! There's been an accident!"

Jack Welborn paled and immediately picked up one of the few

telephones in town. He spoke quickly to the operator and was directed to Green's office. "Mayor? We found someone dead in the quarry. Come quick, boss," he shouted into the receiver with one finger in his ear. "Okay. Okay. Okay. Right. We'll do that."

He hung up the phone and turned to Roger. "We are both to get over there and stand next to the body," he instructed Roger.

They left the office and went to the spot that Roger had found. There lay 30-year-old Hamilton Daniels, who was an occasional visitor in and around Wahoo. Roger didn't know him, but Jack sure did.

"He used to work here in the quarry," Welborn said. "He was a good worker and then he up and left one day without even a goodbye. He didn't even stay around to get his final paycheck."

Roger excused himself and walked over to some bushes and finally relieved himself. He noticed his hands were slightly shaking, as he had never seen a dead man before, not even at a funeral. He zipped up and walked over to Jack, who was now squatting next to the body.

"Someone had it in for him. Look," he pointed to the dead man's body. "It looks like his skull was crushed in." He circled his index finger over the messy red coagulated blood on Daniel's forehead. "He hasn't been here that long."

Roger felt like he was going to throw up his breakfast, yet Jack was acting like this was a dead rabbit or something. "How do you know that?" he asked, as he tried not to look too close at the body, which by now had a thick stream of flies buzzing around what was left of Hamilton Daniels' head.

"First, I don't see any buzzards hanging around, because they usually go after dead meat after a day or so," Jack deduced. "And there are no claw marks or holes in the body 'cause they pick at it," he said. "So, he's been here less than a day, I figure."

Roger turned and stared into the distance. He spied Regis Green as he drove towards them in his Model-A car with the old auto spraying dust into the quarry. "Here comes the boss."

Regis Green drove to a spot a few dozen feet from where Jack and Roger stood. With him was George O'Reilly, who owned the town's only photography shop and probably its only camera as well.

As Green asked Welborn and Roger a few questions, O'Reilly unpacked his box reflex-lens camera, adjusted it on the wooden tripod and took photographs of Hamilton and the nearby area. He also took photographs of Green, Welborn and Roger standing next to the body and none of the men looked very happy at this chore. After ten minutes, O'Reilly announced he had enough pictures and took down his camera setup.

Not knowing what to do next, Roger asked, "Mr. Green, what should we do now? We can't leave the body like this." He shuddered to think what buzzards would do to a body if left unattended overnight.

"He's right," Welborn added.

Green thought for a moment. "We have pictures. We can take the body to the icehouse and store it there."

Jack and Roger looked at each other. "Why the Icehouse, sir? We have a funeral parlor here," Welborn pointed out.

"Boys, this is bigger than all of us. I am going to call the Texas Rangers in on this," Green said somberly. "So we have to keep the body so they can look at it and the Icehouse is the only place to store it until the Rangers get here."

As Green instructed, Daniels' body was stashed on a large block of ice, covered with a tarp in the icehouse and was guarded by a town deputy.

There was nothing more Roger could do for the dead man. He realized he'd better get to his paperwork before he went home for the evening. His boss wouldn't be very forgiving if he let his job slide because of one dead body.

11

Death or no death, business at the Wahoo Brick Factory had to go on.

*****

CHAPTER TWO:
THE RANGERS ARRIVE

Two days after Hamilton Daniel's body was discovered, Emily Deacon looked out the window in the late afternoon and saw two men walk to the inn carrying large bags. The two strangers piqued her curiosity. She smoothed her honey-blonde hair and adjusted her dress over her swollen belly, locked the front door and stepped into the street.

As she walked near them, she noticed that one had a Texas Ranger badge tucked under his front lapel on his duster jacket. Emily's heart started hammering incessantly in her chest. She had trouble breathing as she walked seemingly placidly past the men, who were smoking cigars and looking around the town as they talked to Regis Green. They didn't seem to notice her.

"So this is the town?" one of the men asked with a sarcastic snort. He was a short, burly man in a gray suit. He looked very much, Emily thought, like a no-nonsense man. The man was Texas Ranger Detective (Sergeant) Louis Tillman, son of the legendary "Pecos Jim" Tillman, a celebrated Texas Ranger in his own right.

"Yes. But we're growing," Regis Green replied. Green looked the part of the town patrician; tall, lantern-jawed and with graying hair, he was a perfect poster politician if there ever was one. "As a matter of fact, a new hotel is going up over there," Green said, pointing to an empty lot off Grey Street. It was Green's favorite rebuttal to the reactions of people when they first gazed upon the Ram's Inn.

"A-huh," Tillman said, not believing a word of any of it. He heard too many townies sprout the same nonsense on his many visits to all parts of Texas to investigate murders, riots and various other problems in his 16-year career. It was as natural for a Texas politician to speak wonderful things about his own as it is for a mule to be stubborn, Tillman's father used to say.

"So this is our hotel?" asked the other Texas Ranger. He was Marcus T. Cramer, who joined the Texas Rangers at 24 after an Army stint in World War I. He was now a Detective (Lieutenant) at 31. Bright and ambitious, he he'd teamed with Tillman on many a case. Unlike his partner, Cramer was lean and sinewy while the Detective Sergeant looked a little like Bat Masterson of the old days. The lieutenant had deep-set, emerald eyes on a thin face and lightly-sagging ears. Cramer carried a long black and ivory-tipped cane, which made the six-footer seem even taller. Like Bat Masterson, Lieutenant Cramer knew how to use it.

Emily walked by the men and into Claire's Closet, a small general store. As she entered and closed the door, her heartbeat started to slow down. She knew of the murder, of course, because Roger had been there when the police found the body and he luridly told her the story in finding it, even down to what Hamilton was wearing. Still, the sight of out-of town cops made her more than cautious.

She had craftily hidden her stolen cache of Uncle Lester's goods under a floorboard in the kitchen under the Benton icebox. She knew her hiding place was as safe a place as any.

Thus far, she had not spent or circulated any of the money because of her fear of being caught and – her worst nightmare - shipped back to Oak Park in chains. The very thought made her sick for a moment and then she remembered of the baby she was carrying. *One more month*, she thought as she looked through the store with all of $15 remaining in her purse.

I'll worry about that after the baby comes, she reasoned. How ironic, she mused: *I have the money now, but I can't spend it*. And Emily was dying to do just that.

"Well, gentlemen, shall we get started with the investigation?" Green was eager to wrap this up and send these two gentlemen packing on the train out of town as soon as possible.

14

Something like a murder was not good for any growing town, particularly while Green was in the middle of luring another manufacturing company to Wahoo. The dead man lying in the Icehouse could sour the deal.

Tillman noticed Green's enthusiasm. "Sir, we'll put our bags in the hotel and then get a bite to eat. You hungry, *lootenant?*"

Cramer beamed at his sidekick, who was clearly enjoying Green's discomfort. "Yep, I can say I do," he answered. "I could eat a darn mule right now."

With Green in tow, they walked into the Ram's Inn. The downstairs lobby was a shabby wooden interior with a solitary counter on the right side. Behind the desk was the owner, Jellison Briscoe, a sour little man with greasy tan skin who got drunk too frequently and often shot his mouth off about his "tenants" as well.

"Afternoon," Tillman said as he approached the toady-like Briscoe, who was sweating buckets through his white shirt, even though it was only 70 degrees and slightly windy.

"Can I help you gentlemen?" Briscoe replied, not bothering to get up.

"We need two rooms. With a bath, if possible," Tillman said, eyeing Briscoe with obvious distaste.

"Only the best for our visitors," Briscoe replied, finally standing up. "We happen to have two rooms with a bath open. That'll be $10 a night each. How long are you all stayin'?"

"We have no idea. As long as it takes," Tillman answered as he watched Green squirm uncomfortably as he stood up next to the lieutenant.

"We are here from the Texas Rangers," Cramer said and produced his badge, an impressive gold-plated shield emblazoned with "Texas Ranger" in large letters above, and the word "Lieutenant" and the state flag of Texas in the center. The badge

15

Always got strange looks even from innocent people, not to mention the guilty ones, Cramer often observed.

Jellison Briscoe was no exception. "Yes, sir," he said, eyeing the badge and hustled them through the quick registration process and was paid the $60 from his new tenants, who also made sure to get a legibly-signed receipt from the innkeeper.

"Gentlemen, may I invite you to The Souther Brothers Restaurant for dinner?" Green said in a flourish, as if it were a four-star eatery. "And it's on me."

Cramer looked at Tillman, who shrugged noncommittally. "Fine, Mr. Mayor. Please give us a half hour or so," Cramer said to Green as the two men hefted their travel bags and left for their respective rooms. After unpacking, Tillman waited for a few minutes for the lieutenant, who knocked on his door.

"So, Louis, what does your famous intuition tell you?" Cramer asked as he sat down on the only available seat next to the window.

"Well, I see a typical town mayor who wants us gone yesterday, a Podunk town in the middle of nowhere, and two "policemen," if you call them that," he snorted as he reached for a silver whiskey flask in his pocket. "All in all, just your typical murder in a small town where everyone knows everyone else and a lot of their business as well."

Tillman took a sharp snap from the flask, sealed the bottle and wiped his lips with a handkerchief before he spoke again. "But there seems to be something different this time."

"What is that?" Cramer asked, always amazed at his colleague's insights when he arrived at a scene of a crime. Tillman could almost smell things in the air that other people didn't, or so the legend went. The lieutenant was a detail man by nature and he was very good at it but he was nowhere as good a pure detective as Tillman, and he knew it.

"I don't know," Tillman observed as he looked out the orange dirt-streaked window to the street below. "And that's what bothers me. There's something strange here this time and we're going to find out, right, sir?"

******

CHAPTER THREE:
LESTER

"Where IS my damned medicine? Nurse! Nurse! Where are you?" Lester Hopewell Taylor raged as he sank back on his sweat-sodden pillow. "Nurse!"

"All right, Mr. Taylor, I'm here," Nurse Jennie Mae Bullock answered as she walked into the large bedroom. The drapes were closed and a solitary but dim electric lamp lit the deep, dark-brown Mahogany room. "Whatever is the matter?"

"I need my medicine, you idiot," he yelled. "Emily always had what medicine I needed and I never had to ask or scream for it!"

"Now, Mr. Taylor. Why don't you go to the next room? I made it all nice for you," Jennie Mae said. "Your medicine is on the table, next to the bed."

"Good." Lester slowly picked himself up and sick-man shuffled his way into the next room. When Lester tired of one room, he'd move to another in his wooden Victorian mansion located on 21 Grey Street which was an appropriate Oak Park address for a self-made man.

Lester started life in 1857 as the son of a village innkeeper in Freehold, New Jersey. He learned how to sell from his father and eventually made a financial killing through a new idea called "futures" in the stock market in 1881. He pretty much retired at twenty-eight years of age and traveled the world on every transportation device available at the time. Lester had lived in almost every corner of the known globe at one time or another. His home was a testament to a nomadic life with treasures and art from Asia, Europe, and Africa.

Twice, women almost talked him into marriage and twice they

failed. There was a child in his past, though. Richard Taylor Entwhistle, his English out-of-wedlock only son, was now almost forty and lived in London. Lester had not spoken to him in at least ten years.

Now at 69 years old, Lester was completely alone. In his pain haze, he often oozed through every day and often felt every new day was not worth living anymore.

His doctors said he was suffering from some kind of memory problem and they were right although Lester hated to admit it. There were days when he had no idea what day of the week it was or if it was time for his medicine. This was happening more often. But, on top of it all, Lester's elbows and knees constantly ached from the pain of arthritis.

I am not senile, Lester thought. *It's just that my head always hurt, too.* "Lying, incompetent doctors," he muttered.

"What was that, Mr. Taylor?" Jennie Mae called from the next room as she opened the windows and peered around the disheveled room reeking of dank air. She shook her head at the thought of this sick, scared old man, waiting to die with no family near him at all.

"Mind your own business, Nurse," Lester snarled as he settled into the clean bed.

"That's Jennie Mae or Mrs. Bullock to you," she answered back with a strained sweetness. Jennie Mae had seen plenty of old men like Lester Hopewell Taylor in her forty-year life and she always managed to win them over with her sweetness. Lester was proving to be a little more stubborn than most; he was a lot dirtier and slovenly as well. Morphine pills will do that to a man, she knew, and Lester was up to three a day.

Lester spotted the whitish pills sitting in a silver, seashell-shaped tray on his nightstand. Sighing, he took the glass of water and washed them down. He hated the pills but they were better than the pain. After a while he would relax in a warm haze, lie on his bed and try to not think of hurting any more. That part Lester liked. However, the insomnia and the irregular bowel movements pained him greatly.

The doctors had tried other pain killers without success and only very reluctantly did they have his supply delivered to his home every Tuesday afternoon. On Fridays, Doctor James Evans would stop by, ogle Jennie Mae for awhile and then do what Lester considered a perfunctory examination.

Lester peered around his room. The massive bookcases were filled with rare and antique books which gave it an air of solidity. The windows were open and the aroma of early-spring filtered in. Lester could even hear birds in the distance.

He waited for Jennie Mae to check and fuss over him as usual. Actually, he kind of liked the tall, Negro nurse who so far had taken his best shots and walked away seemingly unaffected. She was the third nurse Lester had employed since Emily suddenly left with her then husband-to-be, Roger.

"Are you feeling better now?" Jennie Mae asked.

"Yes. I guess so," Lester said. "When is lunch?"

"In two hours," she replied. "We have a very nice chicken and rice dish and a salad on the menu today. The chicken and rice is your favorite meal, I understand."

"It all sounds fine except for the salad. I won't eat weeds." He waved his hand, dismissing her for now. Jennie Mae left and closed the door quietly behind her.

Lester waited until the door shut tight and then moved to the bookcase. He looked for a particular book, Swift's *Gulliver's Travels*, and when he found it, tapped the spine three times with his finger. A sliding door opened in the wall behind the collection. Lester reached inside the interior safe and grabbed a small box that measured about seven inches square. He brought it into the light.

Lester's hand slithered back inside the room, but not before he accidentally knocked one of the books onto the floor. He realized it was not one of his regular books. Instead, it was an old, hallowed-out replica in which he'd hidden his will. In horror and disbelief, he saw the book had been overturned by someone – not him. It was empty. Panicking, he placed the little box on the floor and rifled his fingers one more time inside the book's cavity. It was indeed empty.

Lester was dumbfounded. He would have sworn his Last Will and Testament was in this book, all three pages of it. He saw it yesterday while looking for something else.

He picked up the box next to him, opened it, and there to his surprise, was the will – all three pages -- and he sighed in frustration. *I don't remember putting it in the box,* he thought. *I always put it in the book.* Lester's head hurt again and he sat on the floor, shaking his head at not remembering something so simple.

******

After a reasonably-good Texas-style dinner at Souther's Brothers Restaurant with Regis Green, Tillman and Cramer rode with the mayor to the Icehouse where Hamilton Daniels lay.

"That coffee was bodacious. I've never had such good coffee, I swear," Cramer said while trying to get a conversation going. Throughout the meal, Tillman had been unusually silent while Green talked up a storm about the virtues of Wahoo, Texas. He noticed that they had not mentioned the case at all while they waded with epicure delight through the ribs, molasses and beans, coleslaw and bread, topped off with ice cream and coffee.

The trio almost waddled out to the mayor's car for the trip to the Icehouse.

Cramer also noticed that Tillman did not touch the offered "alcohol free" beer and drank only orange juice. *Something is definitely not right here,* he thought again. Since the Lieutenant rarely drank, he didn't have anything against alcohol, even though he overlooked his colleague's occasional flaunting of the Prohibition laws.

"I understand they import it from South America," Green proudly observed. "It comes up by the Mexican railroad. I keep telling Joseph and Parker Souther they should open a coffee factory here and ship it out. Everyone loves their coffee."

Tillman stared out the side window, silent.

"How about you, Detective Sergeant? Did you like the meal?" Green queried.

"Yes. It was very good. The ribs were almost a work of art," Tillman said distractedly. "Mayor, one question: Who knew the victim best? Did he have friends? Any family around here?"

Green thought for a moment. "As far as I understand, he was a worker at my factory, although I didn't know him. I only hear about the ones who always get into trouble and don't show up to work on Monday mornings," Green laughed. "I talked to Jack Welborn, his foreman, and Jack said Daniels was a good worker. No family that I know of, though, at least not around here, that's for sure."

"No known enemies?" Cramer asked. He glanced at Tillman, who nodded as if he already knew this fact.

Green replied, "I have no idea. You'll have to talk to Jack about that. Here we are. The Icehouse."

The Icehouse was a brick and concrete building painted a bright white on purpose to distinguish it from the other town buildings. A large iron and steel door hung on a massive hinge specially built in Germany. The Icehouse was filled daily with chopped ice blocks from the incoming railroad car and distributed throughout the town by seven enterprising young teenagers driving one-ton ice trucks.

The solid, 100-pound chunks of frozen water stored in the Icehouse were vital to the town's economy and comfort in the searing West Texas sun and occasional plains "dust devils," or bigger pockets of air sometimes called "Texas Twisters." The edifice had survived two near-direct hits from such forces of nature in its history.

This evening, however, it had a different purpose. Grimly, Cramer and Tillman entered the Icehouse while Green stayed outside. They both stared at the body of Hamilton Daniels for a few moments. Sergeant Tillman spoke first.

"Well, he was definitely murdered. No doubt of that." Tillman took out his notebook and began to write.

"You are absolutely right, Louis. Look here." Cramer pulled the tarp away and exposed Daniel's body. "I see knife wounds and a bullet hole here in the side. But that's not what killed him. The blow to the head was the death stroke. See how the blood is pooled differently here?" Cramer asked Tillman, who continued to write furiously.

Tillman stopped writing and bent close to Daniel's body. Even with its grayish-hue, it looked very well preserved. He stared at Daniel for a moment. "*Lootenant.* Look at his face. What do you see?"

Cramer bent closer. "I see an axe or something sharp to the side of the face, some scratches and dirt," Cramer said.

"Correct. However, look at his features." Cramer and Tillman peered closely at Daniel's face. He almost looked feminine. "Plucked eyebrows, very little beard stubble and that appears to be lipstick on his lips," Tillman intoned. "Also, very little sun burning or calluses on his fingers. Mr. Daniels here was an indoor man."

"Right again. I think your initial intuition was right. There is something different going on here," Cramer repeated. "If he worked at the quarry on a regular basis, he would have some other small body wounds such as nicks on his feet or upper arms. I don't see anything like that here, Louis."

"Yes sir. You are right." Tillman stared for a moment into

23

Hamilton Daniel's grey, cold eyes. He looked at the small bullet hole on Daniel's left side under the armpit, then at the knife wounds on his upper back. "These wounds were done after this man was dead or at least dying," he suddenly blurted out.

Cramer looked again at the wounds. "Right again, Louis. I notice the lack of swelling around the tissue here, which means the blood flowed away from these injuries."

"I think we need to talk to the townspeople tomorrow. We should also come back here and look at Mr. Daniels in the light of day, in case we missed something. Then we can turn him over to the local undertaker, *lootenant*."

"Agreed." Cramer walked to the Icehouse's massive iron door with Tillman, who scribbled a last entry in his notebook. With a partner like Tillman, Cramer never had to bother with notes for his reports. In addition to his intelligence, he noted, the good sergeant was also a skilled, three-fingered typist.

"Ah, Mr. Green, we are done for now," Cramer said to the mayor, who still waited outside. "As I understand it, you also had pictures taken of the spot where Daniels was found. Is that correct?"

"Yes. I'll get the photos for you from my office tomorrow morning. Our photographer was very thorough," Green said, relieved that this travesty was over for the moment.

"Good. We'll meet there office at 9 o'clock," Cramer said. "Now the sergeant and I are going to rest up. Tomorrow will be a long day."

The trio packed into Green's Ford Model-T and rode back into town in silence. After shaking Green's hand and thanking him for his help and the excellent dinner, and walked into the Ram's Inn. Jellison Briscoe lurked in his usual spot at the lobby reception desk.

"Detectives!" he called out. "I have a message for you." He handed over a sealed envelope. "Someone left this for you earlier today."

Tillman carefully took the envelope, with the words, "To the Texas Rangers" in red letters on the front. "Who left this?" he asked.

"I have no idea, sir. I left to go eat and when I got back, this was in the lobby on my counter." He stared at the pair of Texas Rangers with lizard-like eyes.

Cramer and Tillman went to Tillman's room, closed the door and opened the letter.

Get out of Wahoo. Your lives are in danger. Only because you are rangers, This is the only warning you will get!

"What have you got me into this time, Louis?" Cramer joked. They'd received warning signals like this before during various investigations, big and small. The big Ranger was not particularly worried, because as most Texas Rangers, the pair were crack shots with a pistol or a rifle, although Cramer liked using his cane on most miscreants just fine.

"That's a good question*, lootenant.* But I have a better one: Who has anything to gain from this? When we figure that out, we'll have the answer to our case," Tillman said, his brow furrowed in thought. "The hard part will be getting that answer and I don't think we are going to get much help."

******

Emily Deacon awoke the next morning and started breakfast early for Roger, who was working more and more hours at the Factory managing most of the daily operations. But she dismissed these problems this morning. Now, she felt better; at least she stopped getting queasy from the smell of fried some eggs, bacon and biscuits.

And come to think of it, Roger had always been an easy man to please at the dinner table. Like most men, Roger had one motto: "If it doesn't move, eat it." Emily followed suit, offering him a delightful variety of main dishes and special treats.

This morning was no exception. As he mopped up the last of the eggs with his flour biscuit Roger exclaimed, "Sweet woman...that was a truly excellent breakfast. Fit for a king." He thumped his stomach with both hands and grinned.

"Thank you, my liege," she ceremoniously half-bowed. "The lady is very happy that the king is full."

Emily handed her man a large bag of fried chicken, homemade potato salad and two apples as his lunch for the day. He smiled and the dimple in his left cheek which attracted her to him was even deeper than usual. He kissed her lightly on the cheek and rubbed her belly. "Take care of the little one."

"I will."

Emily beamed as he walked into the street, made a right turn and headed for the factory. He was a supportive man when he was home, though, she had to admit. Even though bone-tired, he'd come home at almost the same time every day, shower, have dinner and lie with her for on their purple-velvet couch brought with them from Oak Park and stroke her swollen belly until it was time for bed. She smiled at the thought of another evening of them together picking names out for their child. So far they had narrowed them down to three if a girl and two if a boy.

Emily already talked to one of the two doctors in town, and hired a midwife named Melinda Gunderson. Taking no chances, she also visited a specialist in Amarillo on the way to Wahoo. They assured her she was a strong woman and would have many children.

This morning she wasn't so sure. Her stomach ached more than usual, as the child within her was kicking again. Emily smiled. This will be a morning child, she thought. He is always so active in the morning, which was true. Still, she had to admit that since the two lawmen had arrived, the pains were coming more often.

The town doctor, Doc Reece Manley, said she wasn't due for a

26

month.

An hour later the one of the ice boys stopped by in his black and white ice truck. "Ice, Mrs. Deacon?" asked the slightly grimy Victor Wells, whose mother owned the antique shop on Thomas Wahoo Street.

"Oh yes, Victor." Emily went into the house to get her purse. For seventy-five cents, she would buy one 50-pound block of ice for their refrigerator and give the young worker another quarter, a very nice tip. Victor, she remembered, was one of the better delivery boys. He'd carefully chop the ice perfectly and place it snugly in the underside of the device, which would then keep other foods stored above very cool for two days or so. Victor came by every Monday, Wednesday and Saturday mornings to supply his section of the town.

"Okay." Victor said, hardly listening as he went through his routine. He opened the back door of his truck and took out the small wagon used to transport the oversized cube. Then, stabbing the ice with a giant pick in each hand on each side, he lowered the oversized cube into the wagon. As it rolled forward, Victor suddenly lost his footing on a smooth spot on Emily's the wooden porch and went to one knee.

Emily tried to help; she reached for the wagon and grabbed it. But a searing pain slammed through her and she fell backwards. Her eyes watered at the pain and she reflexively grabbed her stomach.

The last thing Emily remembered was Victor standing over her and shouting, "Mrs. Deacon? Mrs. Deacon? Are you okay?"

*****

CHAPTER FOUR:
GREEN'S CASH MACHINE

Regis Green, Jr. looked down from the catwalk on the east side of the Kiln House. He watched hawk-like as the men went about their tasks; firing the clay, taking out the impurities and shaping them into bricks – one by one and all by hand. He couldn't detect any dangerous shortcuts being taken this day by the workers, and that was surprising because the work conditions were so dirty and hot and caused the workers to tire easily. Summer temperatures soared over 130 degrees in even the coolest areas of the Kiln House.

But unlike other factory barons of the time who usually didn't care about worker safety, the Brick Factory in Wahoo was different. Green's fanaticism about safety conditions there – the ones he could control – frequently brought him in unannounced, and up to the catwalk in search of hazardous habits. He firmly believed, "A live worker is a heck of a lot more productive than a dead or hurt one."

The Kiln House was built by Regis Green, Sr., who came to Wahoo in 1885. The enterprising New Hampshire man and his son came a long way from the east coast when he heard news of the special properties of the Texas town's dirt clay. The elder Green took only a year to gather investors and build the plant. Starting with 40 men, he turned out bricks for the growing U.S. economy and never had a bad year, rain or shine.

By 1893, Regis Green Sr. bought out his investors, making him one of the first Texas millionaires in history.

Green inherited the factory in 1900 after his father died of an abrupt stroke two days after the new century began. He was thirty years old then and full of ideas. First, he bought huge tracks of property outside the town and built cheap but sturdy brick houses for his employees' families. Then, with the town's approval (and earning him great merit) he destroyed the wooden, slum-like hovels that infested the west side of town.

Like most leaders of industry, Green hated all organized labor unions. He fought hard to keep them out of his factory so he paid his men very well to keep them satisfied. His regular workers would take home seventy cents an hour and those who toiled in the more dangerous areas were paid and twenty cents more. Other labor unions could not boast that rate of pay for other industries, Green knew, and his largess generally stamped out any thoughts of mutiny among his men.

Green was also a savvy businessman. In addition to the higher pay, he also subsidized their rented quarters in town. This was easy enough, because he already owned almost seventy-five percent of the houses within the town limits.

He was also known beyond Wahoo for giving retiring workers a generous package when they completed their tour, usually more than twenty years. He would hand over the deed to a house along with a check for fifty percent of the rent paid over the years, without interest. So far, nine retirees ultimately became the businessman's best political lieutenants. Three of them used the money to open businesses of their own in Wahoo.

This astute man also worked well with three other town mayors who followed Thomas Wahoo's lead and promoted the town in every way. In 1920, Regis ran for mayor and won in a Texas landslide, 99 votes to 5. He was a popular mayor thus far and in three elections since, he had no political opposition to speak of in this small town.

Yet, the incumbent mayor had no other ambitions outside of Wahoo; once a state party hack once had asked if Green wanted to be a county commissioner or even go the Statehouse; he had coldly replied, "Why? My life is here, not in Austin. After all, not all the whores there walk the streets in dresses."

In fact, Regis was grooming his twenty-five-year-old son, William

Harden Green, to inherit the family business in a few years; he planned to rest easy in his mansion on the west side of town.

He might even make a lasting peace with his sole antagonist, Frank Manstill, who was the area's richest rancher and owned a 250-acre spread northeast of Wahoo on the road to Amarillo on Old Highway 134. He and the old rancher had tangled horns many a time in the not-to-recent past, and Manstill was known for having a long memory.

But now there was this murder to contend with. The Texas Rangers' presence was taking its toll. Green took an immediate dislike to the dark, intense Tillman and his probing eyes. He was suspicious of Cramer's youth and breezy country-boy manner, as men Cramer's age rarely went so far so fast by being apolitical or incompetent.

While a murder might not hurt the town's image as much as a natural disaster, it still was bad press. Speaking of the press, it was a miracle no one from any newspapers had caught wind of it. But that would soon change, the mayor knew.

*****

Roger was leaving his office when he ran into Raymond Needham, Regis Green's assistant. "Mr. Deacon! You're wanted in the main office immediately!" he yelled over the noise of the factory.

Alarmed, Roger fairly ran to the main office to find Regis Green there looking very grave. "I got a call from Doc Manley's office," he said. "Emily had an accident. You need to go there now."

Roger yelled, "Did they say anything about the baby?"

"No, they didn't. Raymond will drive you into town. Now git."

Roger and Raymond ran to the waiting car. Raymond was a good driver, but he drove a little too fast this particular morning. Roger didn't care. His thoughts were focused on Emily and the baby.

Doctor Reece Manley's office was around the corner from the City Hall. Roger bolted from the car before it stopped and dashed into Manley's practice. Before his nurse could react, Roger bolted through the office door and found the doctor. "How is she, Doc?" Roger pleaded.

"She'll be fine. She's strong woman with a strong baby," Doc Manley said to Roger's relief. "She had a bad contraction, that's all. It seems your young'un wants to step into the world a little early," he added with a smile. You're going to be a Daddy soon, son."

Roger took the doctor's words with a great sigh. "How soon?"

"Oh, in about ten minutes or so, I reckon. She's in late labor," the doctor replied. "Excuse me, Mr. Deacon -- I have to go check on her now."

Roger waited impatiently outside with Raymond. The wind in the dusty street enveloped him and he couldn't think clearly. He heard Doc Manley's voice through the open window on the left side of the building. "Push, Emily, push! Just one more…"

"Arghh! I can't stand it anymore," Emily screamed. She shrank back on the table trying to escape the intense waves of pain that swallowed her up.

"Come on, you can do it," Melinda Gunderson urged. Emily's hand gripped her like iron on steel, despite the heavy towel over Melinda's fingers and hands. "For your baby, Emily push!"

"Concentrate and push. I can see the head," Doc Manley said in a calming voice. "Your baby is almost here."

Emily gathered all her strength and gave one final abdominal push. "Oh, my God!" she screamed at the pain that seared through every pore of her being. She felt a wooshing in her stomach and only three seconds later, she felt the baby pass through her swollen birth canal in one fluid movement. A quick moment later, most of the pain subsided and she felt a pleasing warmth rippling through her entire being.

Doc Manley grabbed the small blood-smeared child, turned it upside down and gave it firm slap on the backside. It was a boy. His tiny mouth drew his first breath and screamed. "Wahoo Dan" Hawthorne Deacon was thus born on April 16, 1926 at 2:09 p.m.

Outside, Roger heard his baby's wail and couldn't wait another moment. He stormed through the door and was met by the Nurse Gunderson, who forbade him from going into the operating room. "Wait until the doctor comes out, Mr. Deacon."

Soon Doc Manley emerged from the operating room, such as it was. "Come on in and see your son," he beamed.

"And Emily?"

"Emily's fine, as well," he nodded. "She did a great job and you can be proud. She'll need some time to recover, however, about a week or so, and she'll be right as rain." He shook Roger's hand.

Roger followed Doc Manley into the operating room. Emily was soaked in sweat with a towel on her head. To Roger she looked angelic. The blood and other effluvia had been skillfully and quickly cleaned by Melinda Gunderson and there was almost no evidence of what had just happened. The doctor stood at the rear of the bed and motioned Roger over to Emily's side. On her breast lay their newborn son in a soft blanket of yellow cotton.

"I did it," Emily sighed with a smile. "I gave you a son, Roger."

Roger looked at his wife with pure love in his eyes and then he turned his attention to the little bundle on her chest. Like most babies, Daniel looked tiny, wrinkled and slightly red. His mouth opened as he struggled to open his eyes.

"Hello, Daniel," Roger whispered. "Good you could make it, little fella."

*****

"I guess we're done with this part of the investigation, *lootenant*."

Tillman and Cramer waited outside the Icehouse after looking over Hamilton Daniel's body in the sunlight. They didn't find any other wounds on the body than the ones they found the evening before. The lawmen watched as the undertaker's son, Harry Demmer, loaded the white shroud-wrapped body on the back of a pickup and drove way.

Declining an offer to ride with Demmer, the detectives slowly strode back to town. They probed the spot where Hamilton Daniels was found. Bloodstains were still on the brush, and the body had obviously been dragged through it. A few feet away in some light-red clay, Cramer found hoof prints. They were fairly fresh. Cramer traced the pattern with a small piece of wax which left an impression. It was something he learned in a year-long stint with J. Edgar Hoover's early FBI.

Cramer also found a faded red bandana on the trail leading away into the hills. He picked it up with two fingers and scrutinized it. There were no stains he could detect. He placed the possible evidence in a small, rounded bag tied with a leather string at the top.

Finding nothing else of note, he carefully walked back to where Tillman squatted next to the spot where Daniels was found. "I found a few things, Louis," he announced.

"Good. So did I," Tillman said. "Look here." He pointed to a spot nearly a foot away. "It looks like the slicing of an axe or something sharp in the ground here."

Tillman was right. The clay was almost a forensic paradise. Anything and everything had stuck into the ground. Cramer could easily see the indentations on the ground and there was something else.

"Oh yes, I almost forgot. A shoeprint. Fancy shoes, too. Usually regular boots have no patterns, especially the cheap ones. I know, I've worn a few," he said. "These have patterns on the sides, see?"

Cramer broke off a large slice of the wax paper and handed it to Tillman, who carefully made an impression on the light white wax. "This is definitely the print of someone who was here and judging by the distance between the shoes and the other marks, it was probably the person hefting the axe," the observant sergeant said.

"I see what you mean." He moved to the side of the impression and leaned forward. Cramer brought his arm back as if bringing an axe from ground level, over his head and down in a striking motion. "Probably like this," he said.

Tillman looked, raised his eyebrows once and nodded. "Exactly. Couldn't have said it better myself, *lootenant.*"

Their search revealed nothing else. They canvassed the area again, but there was nothing of any worth. There was no sign of any other prints in the area they could find.

Jack Welborn gave them his version of finding the body. Most of what he said had been verified with Regis Green. They made a note to speak later to the other worker, Roger Deacon, because he was not at work now. Green said Deacon's wife had just "busted a Texas Longhorn," earlier that day.

"So, Louis. What do we have so far?" Tallying up the leads was a game Cramer loved to play with Tillman when starting a new case.

"Not much. Daniels was mutilated after he was killed. That we know. He was probably killed by a blow to the head near the quarry. The pictures Green gave us show the marks on the ground. So he was killed somewhere else, probably nearby and placed there. These are the facts. The rest is for us to find out." He took out his notebook and studied his entries. "Do you remember that case in Abilene two years ago? The one where they found the dead night clerk in the alley of that hotel?" Tillman asked.

"The Hotel Renasseler case? I remember it. Why?"

"You aren't going to believe this, but one of the people we talked to was Hamilton Daniels. I remember very clearly now."

34

"Are you sure?" Cramer was always surprised at the detective's deep memory.

"Positive. I remember he wore a particular ring when I talked to him. I even remarked about it but Daniels didn't say a word. It was the same one we saw last night. Maybe it is a social club or some kind or just a one-of-a-kind ring. It had a big ol' pink flamingo on it. Very flashy. Daniels wasn't a suspect because he wasn't in town at the time. Or so he said," Tillman reflected.

"Besides, we found the killer in that Hotel Renasseler case. It was that James Leslie rascal."

Tillman smiled warmly at the thought. "I found him first, *lootenant*. Remember?"

"That's fine by me, stout fellow. I broke the Clancy Case before you did," Cramer said with his lantern-like jaw thrust out stubbornly.

"That's because you knew something that I didn't," Tillman snapped back, a little too quickly. "Sorry, sir."

Cramer started to say something in anger, and then laughed. "Louis, drop the 'sir' crap. This isn't a contest. You've solved a lot more cases than I have and your experience is superb. Haven't we always found our man? Together?"

Tillman thought over the last five years spent with the lieutenant. He was right. Louis knew his boss had sharp instincts but sometimes he spent too much time poking around in the wrong direction. "Yes, we have, *lootenant*. "Yes, we have."

*****

35

CHAPTER FIVE:
LUCY

Lucille Fay LeSueur sat in the train seat and listened to the click-clacking of the railroad tracks. They sounded almost clock-like as she watched the West Texas plains roll by her window. The next stop was Amarillo and only a few hours away, she guessed.

The 22-year-old blonde dancer at MGM Studios in Hollywood wanted to forget about work for a while. Instead, she longed to be lifted out of the crazy world of entertainment and for the next three weeks would be rollicking carefree with her cousins and old friends. She couldn't wait to see her parents, too. It would be the first time since she left for Los Angeles almost three years before.

Lucille had a fiery desire to become an actress in the film industry. So far, she had appeared as a double for the famous Norma Shearer, and as an extra in six other silent films. But she had not hit it big yet with only secondary roles. Her most prominent role so far had been as the spunky "Mary Riley," who befriends Jackie Coogan in the movie "Old Clothes." It had opened and closed only a few months before and she played the part splendidly.

She had just finished shooting "Tramp, Tramp, Tramp" with Harry Langdon. Lucille considered this to be an improvement over her first appearances. In fact, one reviewer wrote: "She is an attractive leading lady with little to do in this film." It was a review that she would note later as a positive step toward her goal of becoming a starlet and eventually, movie star.

Lucille was sensual-slender with high cheekbones and an angular face. Her hair was styled in the fashion of the day with bangs and long, carefully coifed tresses which barely reached her shoulders. The hopeful actress was in Los Angeles for only a week when she was "discovered" at a casting call. It was none other than Louis B. Meyer who picked her from a barrel of beauties to dance in his popular dance films of the day.

Now, with the new emerging "talkies" (there were rumors they were coming, and soon) – audiences would actually be able to see the stars and hear them. Lucille Fay LeSueur was determined to be ready. First on her list was to drop the embarrassing Texas twang in her voice. She pirated money from her $30-a-week salary and invested in acting and voice lessons. Even her friends back in San Antonio would be surprised at seeing their old friend on the big screen and now, even hearing her with a new voice! Oh, it was too delicious. Lucille was going places. No more dancing half-exposed for leering film crews anymore, she decided.

Popping back into the present, she opened the train schedule to see where the next stop would be. *Wahoo at 4:21 p.m.*

She spied the conductor coming down the aisle and smiled to get his attention. "Sir?" she asked.

"Yes, Ma'am. What can I do for you?"

"How long will we be in…" she reached for the schedule. "*Wahoo?*"

"We usually stay there for about an hour," he answered.

"Thank you." She smiled at him.

He tipped his cap with two fingers and moved down the aisle.

According to the schedule, it was a three-hour trip to Amarillo and a change of trains. For a woman on a limited budget, the $19 second-class fare from Los Angeles to Texas was a major investment but truth be told, she was homesick for San Antonio. She knew a vacation away from her dizzying work schedule over the last three years was the right thing to do.

She longed for a cigarette but even a modern woman like Lucille wouldn't dare walk into the smoking compartment and light up

37

alone. Another hour and the train would stop and she could sneak away to the side of the station and have a smoke. How would she hide this new vice from her parents, especially her mother?

Closing her eyes, she thought about being the envy of all her friends in San Antonio. She knew her friends would want to hear any "Hollywood stories" and her opinion of the recent Fatty Arbuckle case – an infamous Hollywood murder and subsequent acquittal of the likeable comedy silent film actor – and she would definitely oblige them.

Like many beautiful women, Lucille was a gawky teenage tomboy who blossomed almost overnight into an attractive, lively young woman. Almost everyone agreed at the studio two simple facts: she was a hard worker who would sometimes give into minor dramatics to get her way. But she didn't care, for she was going to use those attributes to an advantage in a very competitive industry.

Lucille Fay LeSueur stubbornly resolved to be a star and already had a new stage name in mind to one day hang over a movie marquee: *Joan Crawford*.

*****

CHAPTER SIX:
EVIDENCE

Louis Tillman sat on the edge of his chair and peered intently at the pictures. The interview with the two townie cops did not reveal any new information. They knew the deceased and agreed he "was girly-looking for a guy."

The pictures, however, were far more interesting. Regis Green was right about one thing; his photographer was first-rate and supplied the Texas Rangers with plenty of gory shots of the body and the area surrounding the spot where Hamilton Daniels was discovered. Tillman noticed the nearby sage-brush was flattened as if a body had been dragged through it. There it was: a visual truth in black and white.

Something else caught his careful attention. It was smaller clue but possibly more significant. Louis reached into his coat pocket and brought out a round magnifying glass. He slightly tilted the photograph to get a better look at an area near Daniels' body.

Ah, he thought. *This is very interesting.*

Meanwhile, Lieutenant Cramer was speaking to the lone saloon keeper in town and a few of the patrons. Ten dollars later in "near beer," it was revealed the night before his murder Daniels was in a fist fight with Jackie "Mac" Gambone and subsequently thrown out of the bar after an altercation over piano music. Daniels got the worst of it, everyone agreed, except for the one lucky punch which split Gambone's nose.

Armed with this new clue, the lieutenant hastened back to the mayor's office. As he rounded the corner onto Waters Street, the orange-dusty street in front of him exploded in a puff of dirt with the distinctive sound of a rifle shot.

Cramer scrambled backwards in a front of the local bakery. He drew his revolver at the same time while looking for the shooter, he heard the hum of another bullet right over his head. It missed him but shattered the bakery sign. He couldn't see anyone shooting at him from the buildings or between them; still, the sound was coming from the right.

Another shot rang out and echoed through the town. It just missed his head on his left. Cramer smashed through the bakery door and yelled, "Everyone down! Texas Ranger!" The three shoppers inside the confectionary fell to the floor.

Sergeant Louis Tillman charged out of the Mayor's office into the street at the sound of the second shot with his .45-caliber World War One pistol in his right hand. He saw a figure someone leaning out of the window of a nearby building with a rifle pointed at the bakery.

Before the gunman could fire again, Tillman barked, "Texas Ranger! Drop the weapon, now!"

The figure in the window turned at the sound of Tillman's booming voice and aimed. Tillman rapidly fired three times into center mass of the target, which immediately withdrew into the window. The sergeant couldn't tell if he hit the shooter. Then he remembered his lieutenant.

Keeping his eye on any window in the building, he half-ran across the street "*Lootenant*! It's Tillman! Are you all right?"

"Yeah," he heard Cramer reply. "I banged up my knee diving in here, but I'm okay. Did you get him?" Cramer carefully hobbled through the bakery door into the late-afternoon shadows of the street.

"I don't know. He's in that building." Tillman motioned to the window where the shooter had last been seen. "Let's go."

They warily entered the street, guns in hand. By now, a dozen people were milling about in the street and craning their necks to see what the commotion was about. The sight of the two lawmen holding guns made the crow stop and slowly back away.

The pair approached the building and Louis kicked open the slightly-warped door. The former bar had long since been abandoned by an owner. It was dusty and smelled of old beer and sawdust. There were a few chairs in a corner. Tillman saw the open back door swing closed and ran to it. Cramer painfully half-stumbled into the deserted parlor behind his partner.

As Tillman kicked it open, he saw a black-masked man galloping away on a grey horse. He drew his gun but the horseman was too fast and sped headlong into the brush.

"Dammit! He got away," Cramer yelped and shook his fist as he limped to Tillman's side, his face scrunched in agony. "That idiot almost got me. He came a lot closer than the Jerries did in France," he fumed. "But I don't think he was really trying to kill me because from where he was, that was an easy shot. I should be dead now."

Tillman said, "This was more than a warning and it'll be the last one we'll get." He spotted something on the street. He walked over to it for a closer look.

"That rifleman got out of here like a bat out of Hell," Cramer ruefully commented as he painfully half-slithered over to where the erstwhile sergeant half-squatted in the Texas dirt.

"Yes, but he left this behind," Tillman said. He motioned for Cramer to look. It was a small amount of fresh blood. "It looks like I did get him," he remarked.

"See the blood? You did more than that. It's a deep rich red, Louis. That means you hit him in an artery," Cramer observed, using his two years of medical school knowledge. "He can't last long in that condition."

"We'd better get to the bottom of this, and fast," Tillman said, looking around. "This could turn into a war and we could be the targets." He mopped some of the spilled blood into a small gauze pad.

41

"Louis, for once you're wrong," Cramer archly answered. "We already are the targets, like it or not."

*****

Regis Green sat alone in his office with his head in his hands. *Of all things, a gosh-darn shootout in Wahoo*, he thought, shaking his head.

The situation was getting worse than even the town scion thought. He got a cable from his friend in Amarillo, Don Paxton, who advised him a new wrinkle was developing: a newspaper reporter was on the way to Wahoo and would be there tomorrow. While Green was a sharp and adept public person, he had little experience with the media -- except for advertising Wahoo as a place to live and work which would become increasingly difficult to do under these extraordinary circumstances.

A murder was bad enough but Texas Rangers being shot at in the middle of town? What was next? He was lost in thought gain as Tillman knocked on his door.

"Mayor Green, do you have any idea who would wear this scarf?" Tillman asked as he dropped the tattered item squarely on the desk in front of Green. Lieutenant Cramer limped to a chair and sat down with a slight groan.

Green jerked back in his chair. "Oh, my Lord," he said. "That's what Frank Manstill's ranch hands wear when they are on the trail. It's Frank's favorite color."

"Interesting. And what does this mean?" Tillman showed Green the photograph the sergeant was studying when the shooting started. In the picture was a small lapel button with "MR" imprinted on it.

"Manstill Ranch. That's the button his foremen wear," Green glumly answered.

"That's what I thought. Tell me about the Manstill Ranch and its Ranch hands," Tillman said as he brought out his notebook.

Green told him all he knew about Frank Manstill and his crew. Over the years there had been a few ugly incidents between the workers. Manstill ran a tight ship and didn't tolerate any foolishness. He was known to pay well and take good care of his workers but he also had a dark side. "He's the most stubborn man I know," Green reported.

"Why is that?"

"Frank's father was a foreman who worked for Thomas Wahoo, our founder and first mayor. When Frank Senior died, Frank Junior took over running the farm. Mr. Wahoo gave him some tenant acres for cattle grazing near here in 1883 and he ultimately bought out the Wahoo family a few years later. Everything was all right then.

But the railroad came through a few years later and that changed everything. Frank got a fancy lawyer and fought the railroad for almost two years before losing the case in Federal Court. It didn't matter that the state paid them very well for the right of passage," he continued.

Between my father and old Thomas Wahoo, they managed to persuade the state folks to not invoke the right of eminent domain and just take Frank's land without paying for it. But he blamed Thomas, me and every other mayor for what happened. We haven't spoken more than a dozen words to each other in almost ten years," Green said.

"Sounds like a fun guy," Cramer said through gritted teeth.

"Do you know someone named Jackie Gambone?" Tillman asked.

"The name is familiar," Green answered. "I think he used to work at Frank's Ranch but I am not sure. He doesn't live in town, though. That I do know."

Tillman wrote this down and said nothing.

"We have a potential problem, though, sergeant. I've been

43

notified that a newspaper reporter is on the way here to do a story about this murder," he said with a tired sigh. "I have no idea how to handle this," he admitted reluctantly. "Do you?"

"Leave that to me and Lieutenant Cramer, mayor," Tillman offered. He had worked well with newspaper reporters before and told them little except what was already known. The trick was to package the information like it was real news and to keep them happy with a few obscure tidbits "off the record." Usually the lieutenant did this. He certainly didn't mind his picture in the paper now and then. But Tillman usually preferred to stay out of the pulp press as much as possible.

"Fine. I damned well don't want that problem," Green smiled.

Cramer said, "No, you don't, mayor."

"Just one more thing, Mayor Green. Please don't talk to the press without talking to me first. I've had many investigations that turned nasty because the press got involved and mucked things up," Tillman said. "We don't need that here, yes?"

"Correct. We don't need that kind of thing here," Green agreed.

****

The Manstill Ranch sprawled like a pancake across 550 acres three miles away from town. As Regis Green and Tillman set out for a visit, Cramer made a visit to the town doctor.

"One thing about Frank Manstill: He's old-fashioned. He hates technology, doesn't have a telephone even though he can afford it and he still rides a horse to get anywhere," Green explained. "He's also very stubborn."

"I remember you saying something about that. Something about a problem over the railroad, I believe."

"Right. But that's not all. He refuses to take his cattle by rail car; he still does cattle drives to Amarillo and Abilene, like in the old

44

days. Some folks have been shot at by venturing on his property unannounced," Green said.

"That's interesting to know."

After a few minutes, they approached the gates to the Manstill Ranch. The gate was bleached white from the oppressive summer Texas sun and withered hard from the cold winters. Cattle totted the landscape and on the sloping hills. Cowboys on horses rode in the near distance tending the herd.

A large mustachioed man was waiting at the gate for them as they drove up. It was Frank Manstill. He reddened face was locked in the rictus of a scowl.

At sixty-six, Frank was the still-formidable founder of the bigger version of his daddy's ranch and proud of it. He'd outlived two wives and was enduring a third. He had twenty-five men working for him and on the ranch, which was for intents and purposes was the only working alternative in Wahoo, as the Manstill Ranch was the second-biggest employer in town.

Regis Green got out of the car and walked over to Manstill. "Long time, Frank." He did not hold out his hand.

Manstill ignored him and stared at Tillman. "So this is the Texas Ranger?" he said after a moment with a chuckle of half-mocking in his voice. "I thought yew were all 10- feet tall."

Tillman immediately understood this man and how to handle him. "Yep. Ah wuz ten feet tall, but an alligator got part of me a few years back," Tillman cracked back. "But I 'et him and he tasted jest dandy."

Manstill produced a wide grin. "So, whut brings yew out here, Ranger?" he asked, doling out the words, Texas-style.

"Do you have a worker here by the name of Jackie Gambone?"

"Mac? Sure."

"I need to talk to him about a little fight he had the other night, if you don't mind," Tillman requested.

"Ah'd love to help, but he left on a run two days ago," Manstill replied. "He and eleven of my guys. He went to Abilene with a herd of 500 head."

"Two days ago?" Green interjected.

"What's the matter Regis, getting a little hard o' hearing? I said he left two days ago. At dawn," Manstill sternly answered a scowling Regis Green.

Tillman said, "How convenient. When will he be back?"

"Probably next week. It takes about ten days for that trip and two days off in town. But then, you gentlemen wouldn't know anything about that," Manstill sneered.

"I would know something about that. I did a two-year tour in Montana as a cowpoke," Tillman snapped.

"What ranch?"

"Teddy Roosevelt's old place up in the Bitteroots."

Frank Manstill looked at Tillman with a smidgen of genuine respect. "Good. Then yew know how it is. The boys'll ride into town, have a few days off and ride back on the train into town. I would be with 'em if I hadn'ta wrecked my knee a few years ago."

Green was taken aback. "You mean the crew will come back on the train? With the horses, too?" The mayor could not believe what he was hearing – Frank Manstill, of all people, was actually not as old-fashioned as he had thought.

Manstill grinned. "Yep. Ah ain't the old fool you think ah am, Regis. I don't like railroads on *mah* land. On *yours* they can go where they please."

Tillman saw this banter was going nowhere -- they'd likely end up with an with old-fashioned stare-down contest, Texas-style. "Mr. Manstill, we'll be back when Jackie Gambone returns."

"Better yet. Ah'll send him to yew," Manstill nodded.

"Thanks." Tillman and Green walked back to the car and drove away without another word. Manstill just stared at the pair as motored back to town wrapped in a sarong of dust.

*****

CHAPTER SEVEN:
DEAD MEN

Jackie "Mac" Gambone slumped half-asleep in his saddle as his horse ambled along the cattle trail about sixty miles south of Abilene. His nose still throbbed and his eyes were slightly purple and puffy from the punch he absorbed in his last bar fight. He had whipped that sissy, though, he mused. Everyone who was there agreed with that.

The fight, like most fights, started over a stupid subject: the piano player. While Mac Gambone was not exactly a patron of the Arts, he did know lousy music when he heard it. The Brickhouse's lone piano player, Freddy McGuire, was about as morose as they came, an opinion shared by lot of people in Wahoo.

After all, who wanted to hear some funeral dirge when most of the patrons wanted an "alcohol-free" beer or something a wee stronger when they played cards? Listening to some damned idiot plunking away some lousy tunes was not anyone's idea of a good time.

So Gambone, was finally fed up with the depressing funeral march coming from McGuire's withered and battered instrument, yelled, "Hey, Freddy! Play something nice for a change, with a little beat to it. This is the Jazz Age, you know." He meant it as a joke at first, nothing else.

"I'm hired to play, not take requests," Freddy answered, ignoring him as he hammered away at another European death march.

"Come on. Just play something a little different, okay? That's all I'm askin.' The boys agree with me, don't you?" Gambone turned to his three friends scattered around the table; they all nodded and one hollered, "Mac's right. Yore music makes me want to shoot a cow or somethin', you know, put it out of its misery."

The other men laughed while Freddy's face turned a hue of red. He stubbornly continued.

Gambone shrugged his shoulders and looked at his cards. At thirty years of age, he had traveled many a dirt trail since he was a teenager. He was a scarred veteran of many a ranch and all points in between. Mac usually never looked for fights but if there ever was a fight magnet, he was it. On many a night, his bed wound up being a straw mat at the local sheriff's office in the local hoosegow because of too much whiskey, not enough money and lousy cards. Tonight it looked like much of the same.

Gambone was losing his shirt in a hot poker game and not in a good mood when Daniels sashayed into the bar and announced, "Between the music and me, one of us has to go."

Mac yelled, "Then you go, queer-steer," and the boys roared at that one.

It was a known fact that Hamilton Daniels was as close to a male prostitute as Wahoo would ever have. To say that he stuck out like a sore thumb there would be a Texas-sized understatement. Daniels was an early traveler of the Texas underground gay world at that time, flitting from town to town but never putting down any roots anywhere for long.

Daniels' full lips, blond hair and squinty green eyes gave many a female the wrong idea until he spoke and revealed himself as a "dandy-man," as folks called homosexuals in the 1920's. He also made an occasional dollar modeling for newspaper advertising while wearing a new hat or suit.

He was hiding out in Wahoo now because of a problem in Houston a few months earlier. The wife had walked in on the two of them just before things got heated up and all chaos erupted. It was a massive scandal and Daniels had to leave town quickly. Later he found out through a friend to beware: the brother of his latest near-conquest was looking for him.

Daniels rolled his eyes. "Oh, behave yourself. I hate the music as much as you do."

"Screw you, Danny-boy," one of the ranch hands cackled. More laughter erupted.

"I would *love* that but only if you stinky boys took a bath…with me," Daniels replied, blowing them a *faux* kiss.

"How would you like my fist on your fairy face?" Mac yelled, getting into the game of 'bait the fag.'

"Actually, I'd like your fist, but not in my face," Daniels snickered as he turned his back to the men and raised his rear end. "Oohh…baby."

No one spoke. Every jaw in the place immediately fell a helpless victim to gravity. Even Freddy stopped playing.

Mac lost all control. "You scummy fag!" he shouted, jumping to his feet. He lunged at Daniels, who whipped around quickly but not fast enough. Mac snapped his head back with a jarring right jab. The other men were out of their chairs and egged Mac on as he advanced on Daniels.

"Get him! Give him a whuppin', Mac!"

But Hamilton Daniels had survived many a fight in his time on the mean streets of Houston, Dallas and especially Austin. He knew to back up and let his attacker get off balance and then strike.

He saw his chance when Mac half-stumbled over a chair in a rush to hit him again. He swung a hard left hand into Gambone's nose. Blood flew in all directions.

"Sumbitch!" Mac screamed as he backed up and put his hand to his nose. "I think you broke it!"

Daniels circled to the left and waited for another shot. Gambone took the bait but at the last moment he shoved a chair at Daniels,

50

whose turn this time was to be off balance. Gambone's next punch landed squarely on Daniels' chin and he collapsed on the floor, unconscious.

Mac made it to Doc Manley's office and anted up six dollars to look at his nose and face. "Nope, it ain't busted, just bruised a little," the internist said. He gave Mac a small vial of pills for another two dollars and told him to take them when it "hurts real bad, son."

The very same pills now had him in a half-fog as he trudged along on his horse in the late evening sky. Tonight was an all-nighter on the trail because to take advantage of the full moon and clear Texas skies. Tomorrow they would ride until early afternoon and then let the cattle graze while the men rested for the last one-day ride into Abilene. Then payday, two days off and back to Abilene.

His head lolled in the saddle and his horse ambled slowly along. At that moment a loud boom echoed in the distance to the south. The noise spooked the cattle, and one by one, they began to instinctively stop, turn and run away from it.

Mac was awake when he heard the cattle rushing past him. He whipped his tired horse and tried to stop the emerging stampede, but it was too late. Gaining momentum, the cattle stormed past him like he wasn't even there, their eyes wild in fear. This was a cattleman's worst nightmare, hundreds of tons of beef on the hoof charging insanely in all directions and only quick action could stop it.

Charging hard, Gambone raced to turn the flank of the steers and cows. He was just at that point when his horse hit something and stumbled. The cattleman pitched forward and hit the ground hard, rolled and half-rose to his feet.

He howled in pain and clutched his right arm when the first steer plowed into him and threw him back again. Before he could stand, another steer ran over him, stepping on his ribs with tons of frightened force. The blow broke his ribs and he screamed again. His horse was nowhere to be seen.

51

Wildly, Mac Gambone tried to stand but his last view on earth was of a blur in the moonlight heading right at him, flanks heaving and eyes white-bright. He got to his knees and scrambled to his right in a mad attempt to get away.

The escaping steer veered straight at him like a bullet and hit him squarely in the chest. The impact threw him in the air into the storming animals still swarming in panic.

An hour later, one of the cattlemen spotted the dead horse -- and a moment later he found the broken and bloody body of Mac Gambone.

*****

CHAPTER EIGHT:
TEXAS TWISTERS

Lieutenant Marcus T. Cramer had his knee propped up on an old wooden chair as he looked over some notes. The chair only had three legs, with the fourth made from tin cans fastened atop one another. Every time the cans shifted, Cramer grimaced.

Doc Manley said there was no break, just a slight chip in the femur bone. It still ached like the Dickens, and the hurting Ranger almost longed for a liquid painkiller. He sighed and knew that was not to be, as he had promised his Irish mother he would never, ever drink the devil's brew.

In the sitting room at the mayor's cramped outer office, Roger Deacon stood with his hands clenching and unclenching at his sides. He had never even spoken to a police officer before. When Raymond told him the detective wanted to talk to him, Roger didn't know what to think at first. Then he realized it was about the body he and Jack had found. At least, that's what he hoped.

Emily and little Daniel were okay, he knew. According to the Doc, Emily would be out of bed in a day or so and would "give you lots of children, Mr. Deacon. She's strong as an ox." Melinda Gunderson was proving her Norwegian efficiency and was also a major help in showing Emily the ways of taking care of a baby.

He smiled at the thought of his wife and new-born son and it made him feel a lot better about standing in this office and waiting to talk to a Texas Ranger, of all things.

Cramer's door opened and the officer stood there on one crutch. "Come on in, Mr. Deacon." Roger sat down and winced as the Texas Ranger hobbled awkwardly to his chair.

At Cramer's urging, Roger reported what transpired the day he found Hamilton Daniel's body. Cramer nodded and looked up and made some notes until Roger finished telling Cramer about his conversation with Jack Welborn.

"Wait a second," Cramer interrupted. "You went into Welborn's office and told him there had been, in your words, 'an accident.' And Welborn called Mr. Green and said something about a dead body? Is that what you are telling me, Mr. Deacon?"

Roger was flustered for a moment. Then he thought hard. "Yes. I told him there was an accident and that's what he told Mr. Green. I was right there."

"Mr. Deacon, think about this for a moment. Are you sure that's what happened in Welborn's office and what he said?"

"Yes sir. I am sure, at least as sure as I can be," Roger declared.

"All right. Let's move on." *Wait until Louis hears this*, Cramer thought. The lieutenant grilled Roger some more about the condition of body and what he saw. Roger dutifully relayed all the details to Cramer, one by one. The sleuth was confident Roger Deacon was telling the truth -- at least about finding the body and his actions after that.

Although young in years, the lieutenant was a veteran criminal investigator. He'd grilled too many suspects and witnesses over the years and he had an instinct for detecting when people were lying or telling the truth. *More than likely, Roger Deacon was being honest about Welborn,* he decided.

Cramer took the next step in his usual way: he decided to delegate to Louis the task to check on new leads while he, the lieutenant, explored new avenues of possibility. He grinned to himself, thinking about Tillman's follow-up interview with Welborn. If there was anyone who could poke a Texas-sized hole in even the most rehearsed or false stories, it was Sergeant Louis Tillman.

*****

"All passengers, let me have your attention, please," the conductor announced. "We will stop here for an hour. One hour in Wahoo." They were a mile out of town riding over a small ridge; grey plumes of light-grey smoke from the Brick Factory was plainly visible as the massive edifice dominated the small burg's profile.

Lucille stretched her arms and legs as the train station came into sight through the window. *About time for a cigarette,* she thought. As the train came to a stop, she took her purse and daintily descended the small portable stairs while being very careful with her best heels on. As a dancer, she was very careful with her legs: without them, she wouldn't be able to earn enough to eat, she knew.

She waited until almost everyone was gone from the tiny station and then walked a few yards away into some small brush and lit a cigarette in a very fashionable long, black filter. She inhaled the acrid smoke deep into her lungs and smiled in warm satisfaction. A few moments after her third puff, the nicotine hammered her head and made her slightly dizzy.

She giggled and looked around to see if anyone else had noticed her. No one had, as only three people wandered around the small station. She finished her cigarette and picked her way through the clay and sagebrush back to the station. A man stood there and looked at her, a little too much, she thought at first. Maybe I'll give him a show, she wickedly thought.

"Afternoon," he said approvingly as he lightly tipped his grey-felt Homburg.

"Afternoon," she replied in a noncommittal tone. Now she looked directly at him. He's a handsome man, she immediately thought, sizing him up as only women can do with their feminine radar. He dressed very well and even sported had an old-fashioned silver chain watch that hung in a dapper manner from his vest. His mustache was well-trimmed and his hair was closely cut. A lawyer, she guessed.

"Nice day for a walk," Texas Ranger Detective Sergeant Louis

Tillman mused.

He'd walked to the station a half hour earlier and talked to Pick Withers, the white-haired and at times crotchety station manager. Tillman was interested in digging here because of Frank Manstill's odd statement which had obviously surprised Regis Green.

Withers had told him Manstill's crew had never actually used the train that way, he added, "And I would know it, mister. Usually the railroad would give him a special rate, for such a trip, especially for a regular business customer," he said.

Tillman scribbled in his notebook, thanked Withers for his help and left the station. As he walked, he spied a lovely young blonde woman standing away from the station, smoking. Now she was five feet away. He was truly captivated. Louis stopped.

Lucille flashed him an engaging smile. "A girl can't git too far wearing these," she answered, not hiding her native Texas twang and pointed to her modish Carnan heels. One thing Lucille knew: she had exceptionally pretty legs supported by supple ankles. She thought her legs were one of her best features.

Tillman obviously thought so, too. His gaze lingered on her feet and got up as far as her knees before he caught himself. He forced himself to look at her bemused face. "I wouldn't think so. Allow me to introduce myself: I am Sergeant Louis Tillman, Texas Ranger." He doffed his hat with the genteel air of a man who had done this a thousand times.

"A real Ranger?" she said, truly impressed. Back home in San Antonio, the stories of the Texas Rangers were practically legend. Hollywood had already exploited some of these stories in low-budget single-reel serial films called "Western Shots." Later, the label was shortened to "Westerns."

Lucille had already auditioned for a few of these serials, but so far she hadn't landed a role. "My, my. Am I under arrest, *or something?*" she saucily asked.

Tillman chuckled. "Not unless beauty in a public place is a crime

56

in Texas," he joked. "And as a duly appointed officer of the law, I can say there is no such statute in this state."

Lucille laughed out loud. After three years in the City of Angels, she thought she had heard almost just every line. She relaxed, put another cigarette in the filter and lit up, watched for Tillman's reaction -- but there was none. "My name is Lucille Fay LeSueur," she volunteered. "You can call me Lucy. I'm in the movie business in Los Angeles."

Now it was Tillman's turn to be a impressed. "You're an actress? Have I seen any of your movies yet, Lucy?"

"No, but give me a year or so. I work at Metro under contract as a dancer and an actress," she reported. "I even have an agent and he thinks I can go far in this racket. Like anyone else, all I need is a lucky break."

"Something tells me you will make your own luck," Tillman said as he watched her smoke languidly. He realized watching her every move was a sublime sensual experience.

"So what brings a big, bad Texas Ranger all the way out here?" she asked with a chuckle.

"A murder investigation." His face was serious now.

"Oh, my. I didn't do it," she teased, casting her eyes his way.

"You are not a suspect, Miss LaSueur."

"Thank goodness for that. I'm on my way to San Antonio to see my parents and kinfolk. I'm too busy to kill anyone."

Tillman opened his mouth to say something, but at that moment old Pick Withers ambled outside to make an announcement. "Attention! All passengers! Can I have your attention?" he rasped. "There's a problem with the locomotive. We've got a leak in the boiler and we have to shut her down overnight and make repairs.

"There is no other train coming through Wahoo until tomorrow

57

at 3 o'clock."

An audible groan escaped the lips from the few people standing near the tracks. Unfortunately, this was not a rare occurrence for trains to strand passengers, even in 1926. As he spoke, other people disembarked with their bags in hand. There were about a dozen of them now stranded in dusty Wahoo.

"The railroad has authorized your stay in our local hotel overnight at their expense. Simply pay the hotel bill, keep the receipt and this signed document, and you will be paid back when you get to your final destination."

There was a distinct pause as the passengers absorbed this news.

"Folks, this doesn't happen too often, so bear with us, please. If the boiler can't be repaired, another train will be dispatched from Amarillo. Either way, you'll be on your way out of here tomorrow. See me for the documents for your tickets."

Lucy turned and looked at Tillman. "I'd better get my bags. Looks like I'll be here overnight."

******

Lester Hopewell Taylor awoke that morning with almost no pain in his body. Amazed, he slowly dressed and walked into his kitchen where he surprised Jennie Mae Bullock, who wondered what had gotten into the old man now. She served his breakfast but watched him carefully.

"After breakfast, I'm going for a walk," he announced. "I have to go to the bank and into town. I'll be back in a few hours."

"Mr. Taylor, do you think that is wise?" Maybe I should go with you," Jennie Mae offered.

"Nonsense. I can do my own business," he snapped. "But it is nice of you to offer. I also have a surprise for you, as well."

"Oh?"

"I am raising your pay. Don't thank me, you've earned it. Except for those weeds you want me to eat you're a pretty good cook and nurse as well. Plus you know when I need my pills," Lester said as he doffed his spring coat. "And, I want you to take a few days off next week. I have to go to Chicago for some business with my lawyer, so you won't be needed here."

All of this was almost too much of a shock for Jennie Mae Bullock. *A raise? Time off? Whatever had gotten into the old man, anyway?*

"I don't know what you put in my medicine lately, but I feel really good today," Lester said.

"Thank the Lord," Jennie Mae answered under her breath. Lester did not know she actually did just the opposite; she had gradually weakened his medication almost half over the last week in an attempt to wean him off the addictive morphine. It might have been coincidence that he felt better -- and it was not related to his medicine – or not.

Bidding her goodbye, Lester walked out the door and down the street. April in Oak Park was truly a beautiful site, as the leaves were out and the sun warmed his face as he walked. He took in a deep breath of fresh air as he walked and the more he walked, the better he felt.

He arrived at his bank and asked to speak to his personal banker, Jonathan T. Crager. Twenty years before, Lester had opened an account with $49,000; he had rarely withdrawn a penny than needed. He didn't trust banks to store his other wealth because Lester always figured he was the best sentry over his finances. However, he resigned himself to one fact: banks were a necessary evil.

The florid-faced, balding banker was amazed to see Lester, who usually did his banking business through one of his nurses, never in person. In fact, it had been more than a year since Lester set foot in the bank following the incident where the old tycoon had all but accused them of stealing his money.

"This is indeed a pleasure, Mr. Lester," Crager smoothly said as the old man sat down on an overstuffed purple chair.

"Yes. It is," Lester replied. "Here is what I want, Mr. Crager: I want a $50-amonth raise for my nurse, Fannie Mae Bullock. In addition, I want another $100 deposited into her account today."

Crager said, "I can do that." The banker wondered why the old coot would possible be nice to his nurse. He grinned slightly at a possible lascivious reason.

"Excellent. I also need to get into the vault and check my safe deposit box."

"Yes sir. Can I interest you in one of our new investment plans?" Crager asked. "We have a new product called Certificates of Deposit with three percent annual interest..."

"Not at the moment, Mr. Crager. The idea sounds good, though. I'll think about it when I get back from seeing my niece."

With Crager cheerily escorting him to the vault, Lester looked inside the oblong, grey-metal box and found a notarized copy of his will. He wrapped the copy in a large envelope, thanked Crager for his help and left the bank, feeling twenty years younger and very much in charge.

*****

CHAPTER NINE:
SMOKE TRAILS

Angel Rodriquez wandered along the twisted trail two miles north of Wahoo. Returning from a night at his cousin's house in town, he had unfortunately imbibed too many strong Tequilas the previous evening and his eyes were slightly blurred. Still, it was worth it getting away from the dusty business of ranch hands and cattle for a little while.

The light-skinned, rangy Mexican had worked as a cook at the Manstill ranch for six years and the twenty-two year old knew his way along the trail back to the Ranch almost blindfolded, which was a good thing this morning. His stomach felt sour and his breath was ragged as he walked. He would be lucky to make it back to the ranch in time to report to his spot in the kitchen for the noon meal, so he walked at quick-time pace.

A sudden wind whipped him from the east and he covered his mouth with a small handkerchief. The dust gagged him and he turned his head to spit out the dirt. As he wiped his mouth, he saw something in the brush. It looked like a boot.

Curious, he walked over to the sagebrush. He pulled it aside with two fingers and stepped back, horrified.

A dead man lay on the ground with blood everywhere. Angel almost retched when he saw the blood; he recoiled from the sight, turned and, hangover or no hangover he ran like a madman back to Wahoo.

*****

Lucille Fay LaSueur took one look at the Ram's Inn and was not impressed. At all.

The sun-breached sides of the old hotel were warped in parts and gave the hotel the appearance of sprouting wings like a Chinese pagoda. The white paint was also cracked and peeling and the front porch was little more than a pile of loose and warped boards. Also, the dust and dirt that enveloped this town on even the best days found its way into every tiny hole and crevice.

Owner Jellison Briscoe was not known for making any improvements in the edifice that he inherited from his uncle, an itinerant hotel man who won it in a poker game in 1892.

"Is there anywhere else in town I can stay?" she asked Tillman, who said he didn't know.

A quick discussion with Regis Green disclosed there was a women's "Bed House" on the west side of town. Tillman escorted her, and after Lucy saw it she was pleased and relieved. It was a small room, but clean and tidy, and only two dollars a night.

"I have to leave now, but I will be at the Souther Brother's Restaurant later this evening," Louis said. "Miss LaSueur, I'd be honored if you would join me. I would like to hear more about your work."

Lucy smiled broadly at the invitation. "I would like that too. Your work is probably very interesting as well, I am sure," she said.

"Good. I will meet you there at say, seven?"

Lucy nodded. Tillman smiled and tipped his hat as he walked away to Green's office. He could feel Lucy's eyes following him as he left, and he smiled at the later engagement.

Sergeant Louis Tillman was a hardworking police detective who never really had much time for women in his life. This was a refreshing change, he thought as he walked up the stairs to the office. Cramer was waiting for him and grinning like a court jester ready to explode with a joke.

62

"I have news for you, Louis," Cramer announced triumphantly. He repeated the inconsistencies in Roger Deacon's and Welborn's statements. He read from his precise notes as Tillman listened, and nodded at this news.

"That *is* interesting. It's a link to the quarry where he was found," Tillman replied. "I suppose you want me to talk to Welborn again, right?"

"Yes, and I think we might start shaking some trees here now," Cramer said. "Let's see what falls out. Well. What is this?" Cramer said as he peered out of the sand-speckled window.

There here was some kind of commotion going on. A panting young Mexican was talking to Sheriff Red Woodward and pointing up the road with both hands. Regis Green ambled over and listened for a moment, then looked over at the temporary office where the Texas Rangers were working.

Both men quietly observed silently for a moment. A few moments later, the solemn-faced mayor knocked and entered the office. "We've found another body. Just north of town. My clerk Raymond will take you to it along with the undertaker. It might be the person you shot earlier," Green said, wringing his hands in dismay.

Tillman walked out of the office with Cramer two steps behind him. Sheriff Woodward was talking to Angel Rodriquez, who by now was almost screaming in Spanish and English, "Dios Mio! He was dead along the bushes, about two miles up the trail, Sheriff."

Sheriff Woodward nodded and replied back in Spanish to the distraught man. Tillman approached the pair with his own questions in Spanish. Cramer watched, having no idea except for a smattering of words, what Louis was saying to the man. He watched impressed as Louis put his arm on Angel's shoulder and spoke; Angel nodded in reply.

Tillman took out his notebook, wrote something down and gave it to Rodriquez. The young Mexican tipped his hat at Louis and

63

walked to the car where Raymond was standing, ready to drive.

Sheriff Red Woodward focused his attention on the two Rangers to sense their reaction to this latest problem.

Tillman turned to Cramer. "Interesting. Mr. Angel Rodriquez here, who found the new body, says he knows who it is. And since he works at the Manstill Ranch as a cook, he knows almost everyone else who works there."

Now Cramer was curious. "What did you say to him to calm him down? He was one excited Mexican jumping bean. And what was the note for?"

"I told him that he did the right thing; he was not in trouble," Tillman replied. "And that we would have to talk to him later. I told him he can ride with us to the body and take the note with him to give to Frank Manstill so he won't get in trouble for being late."

"That also gives a reason to see Mr. Manstill again," Cramer remarked. This should be an interesting trip."

*****

Wesley Oliver Holmes III was almost born with newsprint in his blood. A Yankee from New York, he migrated out west in 1919 after his tour in the US Army as a journalist and photographer was over. He graduated from New York City College with his degree and had written for more than a few newspapers since.

However, as the slender, lightly-mustachioed 29-year-old sat on this train heading west to Wahoo, Holmes knew he was on to a good story. He begged his editor at the Austin Daily Telegraph to allow Holmes go there after a friend of his in town sent him a telegram telling of the murder of Hamilton Daniels earlier that week. His editor readily agreed just to get Holmes out of the newsroom for a while.

Two days later, he was on his way to Wahoo to investigate and try to get a really good, career-reviving story. At this point in his newspaper career, Holmes could sure use one meaty piece in his newspaper. Lately, his editor had relieved him of his regular beat as a city reporter and had relegated him to the lowly role of assistant city editor which although it was a promotion, was a boring, thankless task.

Holmes loved the hubbub of the newsroom at deadline, but he loved being in the action out of the office even more. After a series of articles about the late-night activities of certain politicians gallivanting around Austin at night, his boss had slapped him on the shoulder and "promoted" him. In fact, his boss had done that as a sop to his friends that Holmes had put in his articles and had almost slandered.

Although he had good writing skills and talent, Holmes had two big flaws: first, he had a nasty habit of offending almost everyone around him with his arrogant manners and a perpetual sneer. Second, he had no concept of politics at all -- especially of the "Good Ole Boy" network that existed around him. These two traits helped make his career a lot rougher than necessary.

But there was one secret the journalist kept hidden: Holmes was a marijuana smoker in a time when it wasn't illegal but it was nevertheless frowned upon by members of society.

His fondness for the green leaf that he bought from local Mexicans had affected his judgment more than a few times. It had helped, along with his arrogant attitude, to get him fired from three out of his last four newspaper stints. Although newspaper people are sometimes nomads by nature, Holmes had almost taken that to an extreme.

Now he was heading to Wahoo with his camera bag and typewriter, just like the old days on "The Front." He felt energized and was filled with anticipation. He was getting out of the office and doing some real reporting for a change and Wahoo, Texas was just the perfect place to start.

******

CHAPTER TEN:
THE ICEHOUSE

Texas Ranger Lieutenant Marcus T. Cramer scowled deeply as he ambled along on the dusky path early the next morning to the Icehouse. His sour mood had nothing to do with his knee, though. The pills Doc Manley had given him had dulled the pain out of as he walked slightly slower than his normal pace. His trademark cane plotted each careful step.

What inked him this morning was the fact that he knocked on Louis' door earlier that morning with no response. Louis also hadn't made it to the communal shower down the hall. The lieutenant had diligently worked the case until the wee hours until he finally went to sleep, notes in hand.

Cramer wanted to report his findings to Louis: First, he had news about his previous evening's discussion with Regis Green, who appeared distraught about a newspaper reporter coming into Wahoo and second, because he was anxious to relay another piece of information that Louis might find a little interesting: Jackie "Mac" Gambone was dead, killed in a stampede yesterday.

As Cramer drew closer to the Icehouse, what came into view was not the burly figure of Louis Tillman, but instead, the sullen, half-awake figure of Wahoo Town Deputy Don Peterson. The officer sat propped up against the wall with a chair under his rear end and his weapon relaxed across his knees. He did not bother to stand when Cramer appeared.

"Your buddy is inside," he muttered laconically with a wave of his rifle towards the entrance to the Icehouse.

"Thanks," Cramer said trying to disguise his distaste for one of Sheriff Woodward's finest as he stepped through the door.

Louis was stooped over the body of the man found in the field by Angel Rodriquez. His coat was off and his sleeves were rolled up. It was jarringly cold inside but it did not seem to bother him.

"Ah. *Lootenant*," he said. "I thought I'd get an early start." Tillman had freshly-ironed shirt and a narrow Texas string tie on this morning. His hair was glistening in the overhead light.

Cramer's annoyance melted away at that point. *Leave it to Louis*, he thought. Still, he had an information ace up his sleeve and he couldn't wait a moment longer. "Mac Gambone is dead, Louis. He was killed in a stampede north'a Abilene. Regis Green got a telephone call last night from the Abilene Sheriff."

He waited for an answer.

"I know. I heard about it this morning," Tillman said, never taking his eyes off the corpse. I also heard something else, too, sir – the locals are calling this place the Death House now because of all the bodies *ensconced* in here lately," he chuckled.

Cramer should have been surprised, but he wasn't. He'd seen the same thing too many times before as the Sergeant had an absolutely mystical ability to "beat him to the punch." It was an annoying habit, but professionally, the lieutenant could not complain. After all, this same Ranger had solved many impossible crimes by himself, with or without Cramer. Tillman's skills allowed the lieutenant to become "noticed" and ultimately promoted to the more visible position as a field officer.

He sighed. "Okay. I found out last night, so technically I knew it before you did," he argued.

"Sounds fine to me, sir."

Cramer stared at Tillman, who went about scrutinizing the dead man.

But something was still very wrong. Usually Tillman would've argued the point mercilessly, taking philosophical pot shots and walk down all logical avenues of possibility. Now he didn't even seem to care. He thought about this morning and wondered where Louis was, but, it was not his business to ask Louis about his off hours.

"Is there something wrong, *lootenant?*" Louis asked. He stared quizzically at the lieutenant. He was also just as surprised that his boss did not argue as well.

"No," Cramer acted distracted, which he in fact was at the moment. He noticed the communal shower was dry this morning; Tillman was a notorious early riser and would always use the shower first. *Yet now he looked almost fresh as a daisy, so where did he take the shower?* Cramer wondered.

"What have you seen so far this fine morning?" Cramer asked Louis with a jocular note. Better to concentrate on the matter at hand, he decided.

"Yes. The body. The deceased is as what we thought and saw yesterday." He motioned Cramer over. "He was shot and he died shortly afterwards. He fell off the horse as he blacked out and that explains these injuries." He pointed to the bruises. His gun was taken out of the holster by someone, too. We also know something else," he said, pausing for a moment.

"What's that?"

"He wasn't a ranch hand. His hands are too soft, no calluses, no nicks, no bruises, no nothing that says he wrassled cattle for a living. Look for yourself, *lootenant.*"

Louis was right. The man's hands, arms and legs were devoid of any marks at all. He also had some strange kind of powder on his face, which Louis had already scraped into a small pouch. "Are you thinking what I am thinking, Louis?" he said.

"Yes sir. This is another one of The Hotel Renasseler bunch. But I wonder, if that's the case, why did Angel Rodriquez say he knew the guy as a ranch hand?"

68

"I think that's a matter for Mr. Frank Manstill to answer," Cramer announced. "And we have to talk to Welborn again, too." He paused. "I think I'll talk to Welborn and you get on up to Manstill's. You both seemed to hit it off, according to Regis Green," he added with a smirk.

"Okay, *lootenant*. I will get up there after I finish here. If I find anything else on this body, I'll tell you."

******

Emily recovered quickly from little Daniel's birth. Within two days she was almost walking normally again. With Melinda Gunderson's expertise, she'd almost mastered breast feeding, diaper changing and the myriad of other duties that new mothers must learn quickly.

Little Daniel was a very well-behaved baby. He was healthy and best of all he would only wake up once a night for his next meal and then would doze until mid-morning.

Melinda remarked about Daniel's sleeping habits. "My sister's kids were up all hours of the night," she told Emily. Melinda was a widower whose husband died three years before. "That's why I want to be my own woman on and eventually become a real doctor."

Now Emily felt good enough to go on a short walk with Melinda and Daniel. Roger had proudly built a "custom designed" baby carriage with some expert help from some of the men at the Factory. They all presented it to her two days after Daniel's birth. She broke out in tears when she saw the pram the first time. Although it looked like it had been strung together with all sorts of odd shapes and sizes and colors of wood, to Emily it was beautiful.

Emily was basking in her new-found respectability. She was a woman of means who had a nurse, a nice house and a caring husband with a future. *Now, no one could ever look down their noses at me like they did in Oak Park*, she thought. The short stroll with her nurse and baby in the warm Texas sunshine earlier that morning lifted her spirits.

Emily Deacon felt completely at peace with her new home and baby. She carefully forgot about the nightmare days when she cared for Uncle Lester and his domineering ways.

"I'm outside with the baby, Emily," Melinda called out through the doorway.

"I'll be right there." She looked for her purse and opened her wallet. There were only three dollars in it. Automatically, Emily went to the icebox and moved it about two inches to the right. For the first time since coming to Wahoo, Emily reached down and moved a plank away and pulled out a wad of bills. She popped two out two twenty-dollar bills for herself and a ten for Melinda.

As Emily put the remaining bills back, Melinda suddenly walked into the kitchen. "We forgot a small blanket for the..." she stopped as she caught Emily stooped over the open floorboard.

Emily froze but was quick with her answer. "I always put a little away for later," she said slyly. "My Roger is just *so* terrible with money, bless his heart." Emily slid the plank back and nudged the icebox into place. "Don't you think it's wise to save a little?" she asked meekly with a smile.

"Sure. Except I use a bank," Melinda answered with a slight frown. "It's a lot easier that way."

*****

CHAPTER ELEVEN:
LUCY LEAVES

Lucy's bags descended with a muffled thud as she dropped them on the platform at the train station. The load was an easy burden to shed, unlike the one she carried in her heart from the night before: Louis Tillman was still on Lucy's mind. She craned her neck looking for him over the heads of the other passengers who had also been stranded in Wahoo. He wasn't there.

Sighing and disappointed, she slipped away to help stifle the niggling thoughts by enjoying one more cigarette before the trip to Amarillo.

Earlier that day, Lucy sent her parents a telegram to tell them about the delayed arrival. She was relegated to sending one because her father was adamant about telephones: he hated the instruments. "Not in my house, no sir," he blasted. "If God had wanted us all to talk to each other like that, he would have given us antenna or whatever they use these days."

On the other hand, Richard LeSueur had no problem using a radio. He could sit back at night on his porch and listening to far-away baseball games from Chicago and Boston and New York as the crickets chirped in his own backyard with a cup of Chicory Bean Coffee in his hand.

He was also known to sneak away to catch and every one of Lucy's motion pictures at the nearby movie house. He'd brag to his friends afterwards, "That's my girl. She's going to be big one day, just you see."

She shook her head at the paradox and smiled as she lit her cigarette. *Good old Dad. He's proud of me, I know it. So why can't he say it to me? Why does he have to be such a stubborn man?*

71

Her thoughts were interrupted by Louis appearing out of nowhere. He was almost out of breath for he'd actually dashed to the station to catch her there. She nearly dropped her cigarette in surprise. Now she spied him nervous over almost missing her and wiping his forehead in the early-morning heat.

"I thought you would still be here," he said, feigning nonchalance. "The train is running late, I heard. I thought you would like some company." As the previous evening, he spoke in a staccato style and not his usual even and measured tones which had spooked many a murder suspect.

"Oh yes. I would like that very much. How much time do we have?"

"Almost an hour. It'll be here at noon. Your connection in Amarillo is late, too.. You won't have a problem changing trains to get to your parent's *casa.*"

"You think of everything, don't you Louis?" she smiled and did a small curtsey. "I thank you for that information."

"You are most welcome." He tipped his hat in return. Anyone watching would have assumed they had just met and were exchanging pleasantries. But nothing could be further from the truth. In fact, they could scarcely hide their new-found mutual affection.

No one would've surmised the pair had walked arm in arm through the streets of tiny Wahoo the evening before. They laughed at some of the dilapidated buildings Regis Green had not bought up and repaired, not to mention the old mule pen and various other farm artifacts scattered everywhere. Everyone in Wahoo agreed something had to be done about those two eyesores in town.

Still, for them, the little stroll had been nostalgic for both had grown up in towns like Wahoo. Louis remarked about how the Icehouse reminded him of a similar place near his home. Lucy said her town had a stable where she would go for hours and help with the horses. The kind, gentle owner, Joe Wren, had been very nice to Lucy. He had even paid her handsomely for that first job, she remembered.

Finally, the magic time was over. Louis walked her back to her room and was silent the last few yards of their journey. Lucy could not believe she was happy and at ease with this man one moment and suddenly nervous the next. She knew she would kiss him but he had to make the first move.

Louis, despite his feelings for Lucy, solved the problem. "Here is my card. It has a telephone number on it. If I'm not there, they can reach me by telegram. Call me anytime. I really enjoyed your company, Lucy – I mean, *Joan*. I believe you will go far in life." He smiled warmly at her but his heart was slowly breaking in his chest.

Louis knew he could not abandon his career to dash off to Hollywood with this woman, no matter how much she overpowered his thoughts. After all, he was a Texas Ranger and that was his job and he knew she would never do the same for him and in fact he did not expect her to. It was a tragic tradeoff.

Down deep, she knew the same thing. And like Louis, her heart was as torn as the decision she had to make and it would be the right one *for now*.

Lucy stepped forward and stared at him. She moved to him and hugged him like a brother. "Oh, Louis," her voice cracked slightly, "Do take care of yourself. You are a wonderful man doing an honorable job." She stepped back away from him. Her eyes were already brimming with tears, real ones, and not the fake beads her acting coach had already taught her in Los Angeles.

He couldn't look at her beautiful angular face with these tears frothing at the corners of her eyes. "You have to remember one thing, though: *'Fame is the wicked daughter of pride.'* Beware."

The words kept the tears from coming. "Who said that? Oscar Wilde?"

"No. I just did."

73

The spell had broken. She felt better listening to him. "Well, then. If that's true, I guess I'm going to give birth to a daughter," she said jokingly.

Louis looked at his pocket watch. "Duty calls. I have to question some more suspects. Goodbye, Joan."

"Goodbye, Louis." They stood, neither moving for a moment. He tipped his hat, turned and walked away.

Lucy Fay LaSueur watched as Louis Tillman, Texas Ranger, disappeared around the corner of the station. She looked down at his card still in her hand as the last real teardrop of her life fell to the dusty earth.

*****

CHAPTER TWELVE:
THE PRESS AND QUESTIONS

"Stayin' long, mister?"

Wesley Oliver Holmes III looked at the filthy street urchin in front of him. As he left the train, he was immediately shanghaied and escorted to his hotel by the ragamuffin teenager.

Holmes had three large bags with him, which the boy grudgingly lugged along in the hazy afternoon sun. He tipped the youngster a whole quarter for his trouble, who looked at Holmes quizzically.

"No, just a few days," Holmes finally answered, distracted. He was overwhelmed by the abomination that stood in front of him: The Ram's Inn, warped wooded sides and all. He looked back at the boy who stood with the quarter still in hand. The black-haired and freckled kid stared at Holmes like someone looking through a microscope and not really sure of what he was seeing; his head was cocked to one side and one eye was squinted shut.

"Ah, is there anywhere else in town that has an open bed, young man?" Holmes asked.

"Nope. This is it."

Holmes looked back at the dilapidated hotel. "Well, bring my bags into this fine *establishment*," he commanded sarcastically.

Holmes got closer to the Ram's Inn and stopped. He turned around to see his personal Sambu running away from Holmes back towards the train station, waving his hand in the air and yelling, "Porter boy for hire!"

Holmes could not believe this miscreant had abandoned him

with three large bags containing his clothes, personal toiletries, and of course, the box-reflect camera, film and bulbs which weighed a veritable ton, to say the least. "Harrumph," he said as he reached for them.

His next encounter was with Wahoo's own Jellison Briscoe, whom Holmes detested immediately. After checking in and paying the going rate of $12 a night, he asked Jellicoe if he would help him with the luggage.

"Sorry sir...bad back. Doctor's orders." He grinned broadly, displaying greenish teeth almost as warped as the outside of his hotel.

"There is no one else?" Holmes asked, miffed again at another perceived slight.

"Nope. Sorry." Briscoe walked back to his chair and languidly sat down.

So Wesley Oliver Holmes III carried his own baggage into his room and almost collapsed in a sweaty heap under the unexpected strain. After all, the cousin of no less than U.S. Supreme Court Justice Oliver Wendell Holmes should not be treated in such a fashion, he indignantly reasoned.

He looked around at the shabby room and his eyes stopped at the bowed bed and he decided to not stay here any longer than necessary. After washing his face and hands and changing his clothes, the newspaperman started canvassing the streets of Wahoo for information.

Three hours later and like almost everyone else who set foot in Wahoo, he found himself at Souther Brothers enjoying a cup of the delicious coffee. The smooth brew relaxed him as he reviewed the day's notes, sat and looked over his notes.

As far as he could tell, the deceased, one Hamilton Daniels, was known as a shady character in these parts, although it was a conclusion drawn from the townspeople who would just stare and walk away and the quick interview was over. The only thing he actually knew about Daniels was a little more than a hazy memory: Daniels had been questioned about another murder and had been immediately released. That information came out after Holmes cleverly bribed a local sheriff in Austin with a bottle of bathtub hootch he always had on hand, just in case.

Something big going on here -- and he was just the man to uncover it.

After Holmes finished his coffee, he walked back to his room. He carefully locked his door and took out a small box lined with a newspaper. He opened the box and saw his marijuana, rolling papers, a patch of regular tobacco and a pack of matches stashed neatly inside. He rolled a small, thin cigarette with expert fingers, then went to the window and looked outside. No one was in sight below. *Good,* he thought.

He lit the cigarette and inhaled, savoring the sickly-sweet aroma as it entered his lungs and expanded them like an oversized balloon. He coughed once and then again. Grinning like a clown, he exhaled, shook his head and took another drag.

Yes sir, this case will make my career, he thought. *Now to find out the secret about Hamilton Daniels.* His past snooping skills had taught Holmes one thing: where there is a secret, something very interesting is waiting to be found.

******

"I don't know what you mean." Jack Welborn squirmed under Lieutenant Marcus T. Cramer's unending gaze as he struggled to answer a simple question.

"What I mean is this: When Roger Deacon came into your office, he told you there had been an accident. You answered and I quote, 'Mayor? We found someone dead in the quarry. Come quick, boss.' My question is this: how did you *know* there was a dead body? All Mr. Deacon told you was there had been an accident." Cramer stared at the now-proven liar with his big jaw thrust forward. His and jaw muscles were clenching and unclenching.

If the lieutenant looked stressed, Welborn looked even worse. "Okay, okay. I knew there had been a problem with Daniels because, ah, you know…" his voice trailed off. "Dammit. It didn't surprise me that idiot Daniels turned up dead with whut he did."

"Tell me about it. And this time tell the truth. It will go easier on you, I can assure you," Cramer commanded. He looked at the corner of his cramped office and saw his cane. For a moment, some good old-fashioned ass kicking came to mind; Cramer dismissed that thought and listened to Welborn try to weasel his way out of another lie.

Welborn told the Texas Ranger about the fight in the Brickhouse and filled him in all the nasty details. Cramer listened, his head half-crooked to one side and scribbling notes as the foreman spoke.

"Okay. So there was a fight and Gambone had his nose broke. What happened then?"

"I don't know. I wasn't there. All I heard was from some of the boys who were drinkin' in the bar."

"Give me a name," the Ranger ordered.

Welborn gave him three names and Cramer jotted them down.

"Mr. Welborn, I am going to ask a series of direct questions. You had better answer with the truth; otherwise, you will be arrested as a major suspect in at least one murder, maybe more. Is that clear?"

"Yes, sir." Welborn sat in the chair like a puppet without any strings.

"Did you kill Hamilton Daniels?"

"No, sir." Welborn's voice was steady and strong.

"Do you know who did?"

"No." His voice was not so strong this time.

"Are you hiding anything from me that I should know?"

"No sir."

Cramer thought for a moment. "Here's what you are going to do, Jack. You are going to be my eyes and ears at the quarry. Anything you hear, I want to know about it or Sgt. Tillman, you can tell him, too. Is that understood?" The lawman glared nastily at Welborn, who physically shrank away under the Ranger's stark stare.

"Yes sir. I have a wife and two kids. I don't want no trouble, Lieutenant."

"Good. Then we have a deal. And Jack – if I find out you lied to me, even once either now or later, I will personally come and escort you to Sheriff Woodward's tiny, stinky jail. Got it?"

Cramer stood up and turned his back on Welborn. He hefted his cane and turned back around to Welborn, whose face was now pale in dread of the officer's unyielding and not subtle veiled threat.

Welborn gulped.

******

While Cramer was grilling Welborn, Louis Tillman was doing the same with Frank Manstill, Jr. It was not going well. The rancher was stubborn, trying to deflect the barrage of questions about the body in the bushes. The deceased was indeed Jim "Rollie" Crosbie after he was identified by Manstill's ranch foreman, Hector Arreno.

"All I know is he worked here until," Manstill looked at a piece of paper on his desk, "February 9. Then he said he was leaving to go to another ranch. That's all I know," Manstill insisted. "He got his last pay, all $100, and then split. I ain't seen him until he showed up dead."

"Why did he still wear your ranch colors? Most men give their colors up when they quit or get fired," Tillman insisted.

Manstill grinned. "Yew don't miss a trick, do ya, lieutenant?"

"Sergeant."

"Right."

"Back to the question I asked. What…"

"Hell, I don't know," Manstill snapped. "I gotta enough to do as it is. You should know that from yore days at Teddy's Place."

Tillman studied the rancher carefully. He tried another tack. "Did he have any family around here that you know of?"

"Yeah. His brother works over at the Flying H in Amarillo. I thought that's where he was goin' when he left here."

"Okay. That's a start, Mr. Manstill." Louis was pleased so far by the information the rancher *had not* told him.

An hour later, Manstill had nothing much to add. He did tell Tillman what he knew about Hamilton Daniels – "Yeah, I'd heard about him. Was some kinda queer, I heard," he spat into the dust. "Can't stand them, myself."

Tillman also interviewed two ranch hands who were present during the Brickhouse fight. They said after the fight, Gambone went to Doc Manley's and got his nose looked at, then got really drunk and slept in the mule stable down the street.

"Ah know. I was sleepin' right there next to 'em," one cattleman sheepishly reported. "And I can tell ya, he farts a lot. Damn near stunk us all out."

None of the men knew anything much about Crosbie. Their

stories matched Manstill's, who watched the detective talk to his men while he sat in the shade of the Texas heat with a frosted glass of lemonade in his hand.

After finishing talking to the men, Tillman walked over to Manstill. "Want a drink, sergeant? Got plenty inside."

Tillman gladly agreed to the offer of a drink to smoothen his dirt-starched throat. After accepting a fresh glass from Manstill's maid, he took out his small silver flask, unscrewed it and poured a small amount into his lemonade. Manstill nodded approvingly.

"Little bit o' shine, eh, Sergeant?" he winked.

"Just medicinal. Ain't nuthin' more," Tillman cracked back. He cocked his head back and closed his eyes. "Now, that's a drink for a man," he said.

Manstill reached under his chair and produced a small glass bottle of his own "medicinal moonshine," and poured some into his drink, as well. The men sat and drank slowly in silence, each savoring their illegal libations.

Tillman was soon convinced Manstill had nothing to do with the murder but was only at the edge of the crime. Now, it was his job to find out exactly what role Manstill played in the two Wahoo slayings in and solve this very strange case before it became public knowledge.

He was certainly not looking forward to delve into the netherworld of homosexuality where he had to learn "about the love that doth not speak its name."

*****

CHAPTER THIRTEEN
COFFEE AND AL CAPONE'S LAWYER

Cramer and Tillman sat in the Souther Brother's Restaurant after enjoying another wonderful meal. "Stop me before I eat again, Louis," Cramer purred over his after-dinner coffee. He was a Chicory coffee man himself but this stuff was far better than that.

Tillman agreed. "Yep, dinner sure was good, *lootenant*," he smiled.

Cramer groaned under his breath. He was very weary after four long days of investigating and still the case was getting more unwieldy by the day. Louis showed him his innovation, a simple line drawing between the names of the key people involved: Daniels, Gambone and Manstill. Three other names of some half-drunk patrons at the Brickhouse had tattled to Jack Welborn, who turned out to be a willing snitch for twenty dollars from the Great State of Texas' coffers.

Welborn had ratted on three guys who turned out not even be in the area at the time of Daniel's death. Louis quickly pegged that fact after the fist-fight with Gambone.

Cramer agreed. The body still looked fresh, as the Icehouse had done its job in sealing the pores and injuries. That alone helped the detectives to pin down a date of death, a prime concern in any investigation.

Louis had a timeline on two sheets of paper. On May 2, 1926, on or about 9 p.m., Hamilton and Gambone fought. Gambone left and saw Doc Manley which the old doctor verified. Daniels had disappeared only to only to reappear dead the next morning in the Brickhouse quarry.

The only thing that went right that day was the identity of the shooter. This fact was verified by the dead man's older brother, George Crosbie, Jr. He traveled by train from Amarillo and claimed the body earlier in the afternoon. He left for Wahoo when Sheriff Woodward called the Amarillo Sheriff, Don Newcomb, who told George the news.

According to George, Bubba Crosbie departed Wahoo and worked at his bosses' ranch for a month or so, then left suddenly. All the surviving brother knew was that Bubba seemed excited about something.

"My brother said he had to do a job in Wahoo."

"Did he say what it was?" Cramer asked.

"Naw, sir. He smiled at me and said, 'You don't pay no mind. You'll hear about it.' That's all I know." Tillman watched them verbally spar for a moment then stepped in.

"George – can I call you that?" Without waiting for an answer, Tillman continued, "I think you know what happened here, or you know more than what you are tellin' us."

"No, sir."

"Ah, hah. Then explain this: according to you, your brother came back here a week or so ago, is that right?"

"Yeah, I reckon."

"So he was here when Daniels was murdered. You just said that," Tillman said stubbornly.

"Yes, he would have been here." George was starting to sweat under Tillman's grilling and Cramer's alarming, cold stare from the corner of the room.

"Did he know this Daniels fella?" Cramer interjected.

"Can't say that he did," George replied. "Bubba and me didn't talk much."

"Did he say where he was going to stay while in Wahoo?" Tillman asked.

"Yeah. At Manstill's place. Maybe that's where the job was," George replied.

A half-hour of talking to George produced no more tangible results. It was pretty obvious to the detectives that George only knew a fraction of his brother's activities in Wahoo. Louis thanked him for coming in and handed George his official card as he left to take Bubba's body back to Abilene.

"So all we know is that Bubba came down here about a week before Daniels died and worked with Manstill. Funny, Manstill told me Crosbie lit out for his brother's place and wasn't here," Tillman said.

"Well, someone is lying, that's a fact," Cramer added.

"Well--*lootenant?* Any ideas as to what is going on here?" Tillman asked.

"At the moment, no. But a lot doesn't add up," he said. "Louis--what do you think?"

"Crosbie was paid by someone to come in and scare us away; that's what I think, *lootenant.* But it didn't work because we're still here. The first question is *who* and the hardest one of all to answer is *why.*"

*****

Lester Taylor's long-time lawyer was Damon Reilly, who kept an office in a very solid section of downtown Chicago with an art-deco decorated office in a five-story building. In fact, Damon had even met the legendary Al Capone once in Al's own personal saloon four blocks away.

Despite the light traffic, Lester arrived a few minutes late for their scheduled one o'clock appointment. After exchanging their greetings, Lester got down to business. First on the agenda, he desired to have Emily Deacon added to his will and testament and second, he wanted his bastard son in England to be included as well.

This was alarming news to Reilly. In his entire twenty-year relationship with Lester, he had only met the man six times and each occasion had been a social and business disaster. Usually, Lester would come in almost foaming at the mouth and threatening to cut another perceived idiot out of his will. Then he would change his mind and go home, only to reappear about two years later, with the same routine.

However, this time Lester seemed to be a changed man, the lawyer noticed. He seemed calmer, the lawyer thought, and he also seemed very in control of his emotions. It was interesting. Lester even seemed charming on this day. He even thanked Damon's secretary Prudence overly profusely for the cup of lukewarm ginseng tea she proffered upon his arrival.

After spending an hour with his the dapper-clad Damon, Lester made the changes in his will – but it was the last request which shocked Damon completely.

"I want this woman, Jennie Mae Bullock, to also get something," Lester announced after finishing his tea. "I want her to get $100,000."

Damon scribbled down the name. "Address?"

"She is my housekeeper."

Damon put down the pen and stared at Lester for a lawyerly moment. "Did I hear that right, Lester?"

"You did, sir. She has been a real blessing. I haven't felt this good in years and it is all on account of her," Lester grinned.

"Well. It is your money…" Damon said with a lilting smirk at the edge of his mouth. *I'll bet the nubile black Mambo is making the old geezer feel real good,* he thought with a lawyer's cynicism. "No big problem, Lester. I'll do that immediately." Damon acted without obvious emotion, but the idea of the old man and a black housekeeper definitely titillated his libido.

"Damn right it is, I earned it," Lester retorted quickly. "So see to it, please." Lester's face looked as if it would brook no further argument on the matter.

A few minutes later, Lester left the lawyer's office and departed for the long trip back to Oak Park. On the train, he took a long look at the outside. He felt a longing to travel anywhere away from the grey clouds and imminent rain he saw through the window. He smiled when a single strand of sunshine lit his face with its warmth.

Better to die on the road than in bed, the eager man mused. So he put a plan into motion to accomplish just that. But first he would send a telegram.

******

"You don't say." Wesley Oliver Holmes III sat in the Brickhouse talking to the Sheriff Red Woodward.

"That's right, mister. This Daniels fella was, well...a little strange. He liked wearing women's dresses and stuff,' Woodward said. "He never gave us any trouble before, though."

"What else can you tell me, sheriff?" Holmes was on high alert; he sat facing the lawman. His writing hand was itching to record any new juicy information.

"Nuthin' much more than that. We have two dead guys--three, if you count Gambone as well--and a pair of Texas Rangers who won't tell me anything and use me and my deputies as errand boys," he replied, frustrated. "And this is my town, to boot. No one has asked me anything yet. 'Cept you."

Holmes smiled. This lawman had just handed him the scoop he was looking for. So far, Holmes sized this up as a small-town feud which erupted into some dead bodies and a big question that still stuck in his head: why did this happen here? Who did it and why?

Holmes resolved to talk to the two Rangers the next morning to see their reaction to the latest information. After that, he could take some pictures and write a good story to wire back to his editor in Austin, who would be pleased with Holmes' hard work and diligence.

Oh, back to the glory days, he thought.

*****

CHAPTER FOURTEEN
TREES AND SILENCE

William Harden Green, Regis Green's only son, finished the solitaire hand he was playing while his train pushed its way over the Devil Hills ridge into the flat plains of the Wahoo Valley. He was coming back home with a full Harvard law education and a prestigious two-tear clerkship with a New York Federal Judge who hired him because of his hard work at the august university.

While not a physically imposing man, at five feet and eight inches tall and a healthy 170 pounds, Willie, as his friends called him, sported a bookish look with spectacles and an already receding hairline that made him appear older than his twenty-four years.

His hands were normal sized, but he had very long fingers that spanned the keyboard easily and were finely tuned to playing piano sonatas and concertos.

If the truth be told, Willie longed to be a musician, not a lawyer. But he knew his father would never approve. He had long ago resolved to "playing his father's game" until the time was right; then he'd sell the Brick Factory and head back east for good. Until then, the old man called the shots and Willie knew it.

Although he wanted to stay in New York, his father wanted him to come back to tiny Wahoo and take over the family business. Willie was not a fool and he knew who buttered his bread, so he meekly complied. Besides, after enduring a he had a broken heart over his latest affair; he thought a new start back home would be a good idea.

Willie sighed as he thought about his last trip back to the dusty plains. He and his father argued briefly about his taking over the business now instead of later; his dad wanted to retire and enjoy the niceties of older age. In fact, his father preached about that all the time. The elder Green also longed for grandkids to play with so "I can sit in the shade of the trees and watch the people dance."

The screaming match in the old man's over-sized living room that day long ago had so unnerved Willie that he stomped out and got completely drunk; the next morning he found himself in bed with another night-time lover.

Then things got worse. When his nocturnal bedmate discovered who he was, an extortion attempt was made over Willie's night-time misdeeds to Regis Green.

The senior Green lost all control with the smarmy crook and nearly bashed the fool over his head with an iron wrench; he was stopped by doing so by the fortunate arrival of Jack Welborn at the Quarry. No money was paid.

Fuming, Regis Green put his son on the next train out of Wahoo and to New York. Now the appropriate time had passed; he was forgiven and welcome to come back again.

Clarissa Green, Willie's mother, had died during the Great Influenza Epidemic of 1916 when Willie was fourteen. Only one other person died in Wahoo in that tragedy. Like many small isolated American towns, Wahoo was spared during that nine-month calamity that took an estimated million lives over the globe.

It's been ten years now since Mom died, Willie reflected as he gazed at the plains stretching our on all sides of his rail car. He closed his eyes and thought of his mother for a moment and how she had understood him perfectly. While his father could be aloof and standoffish, Willie's mother was a warm and genuine Southern Carolina belle who met her future husband at a tea dance in Baltimore. Willie loved her quiet, gentle style and even though she fussed so much over her only son was understandable, as Willie's sister Louisa had died during childbirth when he was barely eight years old. His other sister, Jeanne, was three years older and lived in Boston with her politician husband.

Clarissa desperately wanted another child, but Regis was very adamant: the doctor said the danger was too high for Clarissa and they never spoke of it again, at least not in Willie's presence.

Willie grew up absolutely doted upon by his mother and virtually ignored by his father. When she died, he was emotionally traumatized for a few years, which resulted in more than one problem with the law but nothing serious. With older sister Jeanne's help, Willie snapped to his senses and resolved to make the law his life.

Four hectic years later at Harvard, he accomplished just that. And what was his father's response? "Great. Now get back here and take over the factory. I want to retire." If his father had been insistent then, he was not nearly so demanding now. "I'm not getting any younger, son," he said in a telephone call earlier that week to Willie. "Come on back and we can discuss it, son."

One thing Willie had noticed, though. His father was getting older and a little bit mellower as well. His request on the telephone had been almost a plea, not an order. Before, his father would have blustered and yelled at him; now, he was gently asking for his son to take his rightful place in the modest Green Empire.

Maybe now he will listen to me and maybe he will finally understand me like Mom did, Willie thought. At least, that's what he hoped as he spotted Wahoo and the Brickhouse in the distance.

******

"Look, I told yew the same thing I told that nut with the cane," Larry Welborn mumbled to Wesley Oliver Holmes III in the middle of the Texas desert at a meeting spot of his choosing. Holmes' eyes darted around in the gathering darkness. He looked like he would jump out of his skin at any strange sound or movement.

"Still, my good man. I came all the way out here and you have nothing more to tell me?" Holmes scolded. He handed the foreman $10 for inside information but so far, he believed he knew as much as Welborn. Maybe the lying coot was holding something back for more money. *Probably the latter*, Holmes thought.

"Wait. I just remembered something," Welborn blurted out. "That Ranger lieutenant made a big deal outta something I told him about Hamilton Daniels, you know, the dead guy. I said Daniels had been in a fight at the bar and then he had left while Gambone went to Doc Manley's office to get his nose fixed. That queerboy got a lucky punch in, I heard."

Holmes was beginning to lose his patience. "Yes, I know. So does the entire town, Jack." He frowned heavily at Welborn, who avoided his stare.

"Wait. Now I remember. This Daniels guy had an affair with someone in town and there was trouble," he declared. "And I also overheard the lieutenant telling the spooky other ranger that he hoped there wasn't a secret society of queer boys running around." He looked expectantly at Holmes, who immediately dropped the mean look.

Remembering his professionalism, Holmes quickly composed himself, grabbed his notebook and began asking questions of Welborn. He was hesitant at first, but finally he alluded to the reporter that a secret society was running loose around extorting rich people's kids. Their method was simple: get the victim stone drunk and take crude pornographic pictures with a reflex camera, then use the damning evidence to finance another adventure.

Welborn even knew the name of the cartel: *The Pink Flamingos*.

Holmes wrote furiously by the small fire's light to these revelations. He continued peppering Welborn with questions until it was obvious the man knew nothing more. Holmes surprised Welborn with another $10, thanked him for the new details and walked back to town.

******

A day after Melinda spied her with the stolen money, Emily panicked. She crept around the floorboards of the old house but there were no more hiding spaces to be found. As there was no foundation as such, there was not a crawl space under the house, either.

So she thought and had a brilliant answer; simply hide it in the Icehouse. Since no one ever locked the Icehouse prior to the murders, it was an easy task to go and hide the money and jewelry. In fact, there was an "honor system" tray there for after-hour customers and as far as anyone could tell, there had never been an ice robbery in the entire history of Wahoo.

She snuck out of her warm bed the same evening while Roger snored mightily next to her. Fortunately, there was a new moon and little light that evening; Emily was sure she was not seen in her nocturnal trip. Inside the Icehouse, she found the right rear corner and put the small bundle inside a small iron trap door used for smaller ice cartons but was rarely used, she knew.

She smiled to herself with her cleverness. Now if Melinda talked to anyone, Emily could deny it and feign ignorance; a search under the refrigerator would reveal nothing and that's the way Emily wanted to keep things. With the Texas Rangers in town over a couple of murders already, Emily did not want to attract any attention.

*****

CHAPTER FIFTEEN:
TURF BATTLES

"I have to take you in, Frank. We gotta have a pow-wow about this Daniels thing," Sheriff Red Woodward said as he stood at the gates of Manstill's Ranch with his two deputies in tow, just in case. After all, Frank Manstill, Jr. was known as a stubborn guy in these parts.

Manstill stood with his arms folded across his chest. "Nice try, Red. Yew know I had nuthin' to do with this shit," he spat a large wad of well-chewed tobacco just beyond where the sheriff stood. The next brown mini-bomb wouldn't be so discreet.

"Come on. You know how it goes, Frank. I take you in, hold you in a cell for a few hours, and then let ya' go, cleared of all charges—by me. Then those Rangers will have to look at someone else. Right now they think you know more than you've been lettin' on."

"Yeah, they aren't stupid."

"So, let's go, Frank. Let's have no problems, okay?"

"Did Regis put you up to this?"

"I can't answer that," Sheriff Woodward averted Manstill's angry and unwavering stare while his deputy quickly handcuffed the recalcitrant rancher. The ride into town was surprisingly uneventful. Woodward's mind had conjured up all kinds of scenarios, but a handcuffed Manstill rode in silence in the back with a deputy at his side. He seemed almost amused by ride.

Along the way, Woodward caught the man's eyes moving back

and forth and up and down; he was examining every detail of the car's worn interior. Truth was, even with all his wealth, Manstill had only seen an automobile up close a few times, and to his recollection, this was only the fourth time he'd actually taken a ride in one.

The retinue stirred up clouds of dust when it stopped in front of the town's three-cell jail. Over by the train station, a dozen Wahoo folks stopped what they were doing and stared at the men. They had already heard the news, which streaked through the town like a wildfire: Frank Manstill had been arrested and taken to jail by Sheriff Red Woodward.

Cramer and Tillman were surprised when Regis Green told them only moments after Woodward packed Manstill into his cell. A deputy was then dispatched to personally tell the mayor.

"What the hell is going on?" Cramer demanded of the mayor. "He's not even a suspect!" he thundered.

"Mayor." Tillman's more soothing tone successfully deflected his superior's outburst. "Exactly why was Manstill brought in?"

"As I understand it, the sheriff wanted to question him," Green replied. "But, you'll have to talk to him about that; it's not my department."

"Yeah, as chief of police, I guess that wouldn't concern you too much," Tillman retorted. Upon hearing that, Cramer grabbed his cane and ambled angrily to the door with Louis in quick pursuit. Without another word, they deserted the mayor's office and headed towards the jail. Before they got to the two blocks, Sheriff Woodward met up with them in the middle of the street.

"Yew Rangers can go cool your heels for a while. Ah got Manstill and he's tawkin' to me from now on," the sheriff reported with a smirk.

"Oh? I believe you are wrong, sheriff," Cramer snipped. "We have jurisdiction here and you know it."

"That's right. You do, sir. But based on the Memorandum of Understanding between towns like us and Austin, we get to investigate first and then you come in. Ah'm shure yew've heard'a that piece of law, right, *lieutenant?*"

Cramer's jaw tightened. The local lawman was right—he'd done his homework. He and Tillman had relegated the sheriff and his men to a secondary role in the investigation. And since Wahoo was not incorporated into a county, the legal rules that applied to it were unique. It was actually just a technicality and a holdover tradition from the 1880s. Still, Cramer knew this was not the way to handle an investigation. Besides, he wanted first crack at Manstill. And he didn't like it one bit that a law from almost half a century ago was still in effect.

"Sheriff Woodward. That is a guideline that we'll all just have to work with. Fact is, you are interfering with an active investigation that we are legally empowered to handle," Tillman argued. "But, we'll meet you half-way. Go ahead and question Manstill. Let us know your findings before turning him over to us."

"Perfect. Couldn'ta said it better myself. Gentlemen..." the sheriff said with an air of finality. Then he tipped his hat, turned and walked back to the jail. "I'll send one of my boys for you," he said over his shoulder to Cramer and Tillman.

Cramer whirled on Louis, his eyes flashing. "Damn it, Louis. Why did you do that?"

"I already know what Manstill is going to tell Woodward," Tillman said, defending his statement. "Remember, I talked to him alone yesterday. If there is a difference in what he told me, we'll act on that knowledge. Until then, we'll let the sheriff have his day and waste his time, sir. But we can't afford to waste ours."

******

Roger wondered why his wife was getting up at all hours of the night and taking long walks. Twice the previous week he woke up and found her gone. On those occasions, he had hastily dressed and walked through the tiny house not knowing what to think. Each time he went to Daniel's room first. The lad was fast asleep, as always. Still, there no sign of Emily. After the second time, he found himself faced with a dreaded confrontation.

Now, three days later, she was gone again. He looked at his pocket watch in the dim light: just after one o'clock in the morning. Groaning, he got up and whispered, "Emily. Emily. Are you there?"

No answer. Roger dressed again in the pants, shoes and thin shirt that he now kept by the bed. Checking on his sleeping son, he felt sure that once again Emily was not in the house. He went into the kitchen and turned on the light. He saw that her coat was gone, as well as her shoes; clearly, she meant to leave in the middle of the night.

Now he was torn about what to do next: Leave Daniel here alone and search for her, or just wait in the darkness for her to reappear? Roger opted to wait. He turned out the light, sat down in the darkest corner of the kitchen and waited.

Twenty minutes later, the front door creaked open and Emily slunk inside with a bundle under her arm. Roger held his breath. Before she could react, he quickly flicked the light switch.

The light blinded both of them for a second and then it revealed a shocked and befuddled Emily looking wildly at her husband. She realized he had been glaring at her all this time, in silence.

"Roger?" was all she managed to rasp at him.

"What in the name of Hell is going on here? And what is that?" he pointed at the bundle. "I want the truth, Emily and I want it *now.*"

Emily's knees buckled and she knew she was going to faint. She gathered her senses and steeled herself, still awkwardly not knowing what to say. She approached him defensively and slowly. Then she crouched forward and buried her face in her hands. She started sobbing ferociously. Roger forced his eyes to close as he heard the confession that came out of her. When it was over, he knew it had been the truth.

Emily looked at her husband and braced herself for the dreaded expression she expected to see. He opened his eyes and stared at her, drained of all emotion. Then he swallowed hard.

"We will have to give it back, Emily" he commanded." And you will apologize. I won't listen to anything else. It's the right thing to do and we both know it. You'd better hope Lester has sympathy for you. But from my dealings with him, that is not too damned likely."

"I know." She sniffed back more tears.

Roger could never stay angry at Emily. He stood there for a time but soon knelt beside her and took her hands. "I will try and make it right with Lester, Emily. I will talk to him, man to man. As long as he gets the money back, things will be all right. I understand why you did it; I just can't understand why you didn't simply demand wages for your work."

"He told me that if I reported his money it to a government office or the tax people, I'd be thrown out into the street. I couldn't go broke, Roger. What choice did I have?"

It had been a trying ordeal and Roger needed at least some sleep before another day at the Brickhouse. "I'm going to bed. I suggest you do the same, Emily. Don't worry. Tomorrow we'll send Lester a telegram and get this behind us. You won't go to jail, I promise.'

Emily melted next to him in their warm bed. For the first time in more than a week, she slept deeply until the sun's rays peered through her window four hours later.

*****

97

CHAPTER SIXTEEN:
THE STENCH OF GUILT

The two Texas Rangers sat in silence at Souther's Restaurant after Sheriff Red Woodward had made his power play. Even the sweet, aromatic coffee could not settle their moods.

"Damn it, Louis," Cramer said. He now tried hard to lose himself in the delicious brew. "I hate playing second fiddle, particularly in this murder investigation."

"Yes, yes," Tillman commiserated. "Still, it's the best way to get through this, sir. I probably like it even less than you do, if that's possible." He took out his silver flask and poured some Kentucky cask-aged whiskey into his coffee while his boss pretended not to notice.

"We have three deaths. Crosbie's death happened in that scuffle with us, Gambone's death was an accident—I don't think he killed Daniels, anyway, because of the discrepancy of the timing. Agreed?"

Tillman nodded. "So that leaves Daniels being killed by someone else. And Sheriff Woodward has Manstill. On paper, he appears to be a reasonably good suspect. But I remember something important that we should relay to the sheriff. Manstill rarely comes into town; he has been here only four known times in the last three years. I think the entire town would pretty much swear to that which alone makes it unlikely—nearly impossible—for him to be the killer."

"True. The town would probably agree to that, at this point."

As they spoke, a thin, dapper young man walked casually by their table and intentionally dropped something on the corner. He kept walking without looking back. Cramer grabbed the paper, which was a small handwritten note. Louis studied the stranger as he disappeared out the door.

"Look at this," Cramer said, reading the words. He handed it to Tillman.

"We have a late-night meeting with someone who might have some new information."

The note said: *I have something you will want to know. Meet me by the Main Horse Stable at midnight.* It was signed, *A citizen.*

Both men were naturally encouraged. So far, the townspeople had been stubborn with information and they had been anything but forthcoming with the rangers. Most just clammed up or rudely walked away from the detective's queries. That made Tillman certain that some pressure was being applied by someone but he didn't know who that was.

Now, this new informant wanted to parley with them. It made Cramer suspicious. "This could be a trap," he said.

"Yes sir. But I think it's another kind of trap, just to fool us. Let's play along and see what happens."

"I still don't like it, Louis. The entire thing stinks to high Heaven."

"But when things smell, sir, the path is always easier to follow."

******

Back in Oak Park, Lester awoke an invigorated man. After pressing a folded copy of his new will into the wall safe, he removed 20 gold coins that had been saved from his trips to the Middle East. He placed those in an envelope marked *For Daniel Deacon.* Lester wanted his grandson to have a chance for a better than-just-good life. This was one way he could provide a legacy, he decided.

He also found some hand-made ancient Inca jewelry for Emily. In truth, Lester felt guilty about how he treated his niece; there was a long time that he lived in a depression-filled cloud as his health began to fail and sweet Emily bore the brunt of his frustration. Now he was determined t right that wrong.

Lester checked the Chicago train schedule and made notes in the little note book placed next to him on many bedside tables during the years of his world travels. Unfolding the map of Texas, he peered closely. He could barely make out the tiny burg of Wahoo, indicated only by a small dot.

Folded on his writing desk was Emily Deacon's letter sent to Lester a week after Daniel's birth. Emily's perfunctory letter to Lester tersely announced the arrival of his grandson but not much in the way of details was given.

I deserve that kind of treatment, Lester mused.

Jennie Mae Bullock finished packing Lester's belongings for a two-week trip. Surely, he thought was well enough to travel by himself, but this time, she vehemently insisted on accompanying him. "Mr. Taylor, I *am* your nurse. My job is to take care of you medically, and you *cannot* leave me here while you traipse over the countryside." Her stern face was quite telling. The old man could see that arguing with her would not do one single bit of good.

"Fine. Then make yourself useful and make darn sure I have everything. We're going to ride to Texas on the first train out tomorrow…"

"Texas?" Jennie Mae interrupted. She always wondered where Emily had gone some months before. Going there now, she thought, would be like going to the South Pole. "What on earth is in Texas?"

"Not *what*—who! My grandchild, Daniel," Lester announced, smiling. "And his grand daddy is coming for a visit. Now, I need to write a telegram, so you just get to work, *nurse.*"

******

The telegram from Lester Hopewell arrived by one of the town's kids who worked as a paid "runner" for the telegraph office.

DEAR EMILY AND ROGER AND DANIEL (STOP) WILL BE IN WAHOO IN TWO DAYS (STOP) HAVE A BIG SURPRISE FOR YOU (STOP) WILL ARRIVE ON SOUTHERN PACIFIC AT 4 PM ON JUNE 5 (STOP) LESTER HOPEWELL TAYLOR

Roger could not believe the words he had just read. He read it three more times and thought hard about this news. *Lester was on his way here to Wahoo? Why now,* he wondered Roger hadn't summoned the courage to call Lester yet, but he never expected this. The prospect of the old man suddenly showing up with a "big surprise" was almost more than Roger could handle.

Emily didn't take it any better. Her face went chalk-white when Roger told her the news. She looked at the telegram again and noticed Uncle Lester had mentioned Daniel, which she took as one possible ray of hope.

"We have to call him, Emily," Roger argued.

"He doesn't have a telephone, remember?"

"Then, we have to get someone to have him call us," he retorted.

"Roger, it's too late," Emily said, visibly shaking and pointing to the date on the note. "He's on his way. Look at the date: it's dated today, June 3, 1926." Lester, the man she had hated so much and stolen his property in revenge, was already on his way to Wahoo and there was nothing the two could do to stop him.

*****

The evening light threw shadows everywhere the detectives looked. Inside the stable, only a few horses were stirring in their

101

stalls. Texas Rangers Tillman and Cramer walked inside with their weapons drawn; Cramer had his cane in one hand and his .44 caliber Smith & Wesson pistol in the other. Tillman had his loaded .38 caliber Black Beauty Special thrust out in front of him, both hands on the grip.

They were not alone. Their informer moved out from inside an empty stall. "Hello?" he said in a plaintive voice.

"Texas Rangers! Come out and keep your hands in view," Cramer commanded.

"I'm not armed." The man stepped out of the shadows so the rangers could see him. "I'm Franklin C. Hayden," he said with his hands in the air. "I know some things, but I don't know why they killed Ham." He was a mid-sized man, appeared to be about thirty years old and was quite well-dressed, at least by Wahoo standards.

Cramer holstered his gun and stared at Hayden. Tillman kept a watchful vigil but it was obvious they were all still alone.

Hayden told the detectives about the *Flamingos*—the activities of the underworld club. He confirmed what the detectives already suspected about a secret society. But what they hadn't heard, at least until now, was that the key victim in the sting operation was none other than Willie Harden Green, Regis Green's son.

"Did Daniels conduct this scheme alone?" Cramer asked.

"No sir. He had help: Me."

Tillman asked, "What happened?"

Hayden came out with everything he knew. He explained the bed partner incident two years before and how the younger Green had been forced by his father to leave town suddenly on the next train. He also told the detectives about the aftermath. "Regis Green almost split my head open with a shovel," Hayden said. "That Welborn fella' stopped him, though."

"Did you contact other people about this?" Cramer asked.

"Not here in Wahoo. We didn't dare with Green's son being the richest guy around here. Ham was here only to hide out for a while. I was in Austin when he was killed and I can prove it."

"I hope you can."

Hayden handed Cramer a train ticket dated the day before Daniels' bar fight with Gambone. "As you can see, I went from Austin to Dallas. I was visiting a friend and I found out about Ham when I got back to Austin. I came back here as soon as I could."

"So far, this looks good for you. But why are you coming to tell us this, anyway?" Cramer asked.

"I want to help catch Ham's murderers. He meant a lot to me," Hayden said, looking down and starting to get upset. "Willie's dad is a mean guy. I know he had something to do with this," Hayden said. "I just know it. This isn't the first time…"

"We'll find out," Cramer answered. "Meanwhile, you stay out of sight and we will check out your ticket. And no talking to the press or anyone else either, understand?"

Hayden nodded. He was more settled and confident now that his version of the story was out.

"I wouldn't leave the city limits if I were you," Tillman interjected. "We still have to check out your story. Is there anyone outside of Wahoo who can vouch for your whereabouts, Hayden?"

"Yes. A policeman. I had to go to Dallas to get a friend out of jail." He relayed the details to Tillman, who wrote this information quickly into his black book in the fading grey light.

"We will meet you tomorrow night here at the same time. Midnight," Cramer said with solemn finality. "Make sure you get here," he warned.

"Ok. I understand," Hayden promised.

On their way back to the Ram's Inn, the detectives silently tallied up Hayden's testimony. If Willie Green had been an extortion target, why didn't Regis Green mention it? And why did he deny knowing Hamilton Daniels?

Regis Green was hiding something. Tillman was right: the stench was indeed making the path easier to follow.

*****

CHAPTER SEVENTEEN:
TRUTH IS JUST A WORD

Lester was bored by the wide and flat endless Oklahoma Plains slowly meandering past his window on the Santa Fe Night Owl. The nearly-exhausted veteran traveler had forgotten how tedious modern train travel could be.

The journey had started off fine for him. Initially, was filled with high expectations for a smooth reconciliation with Emily. But now, even with Jennie's Mae's assistance, the logistics of traveling made him tired and irritable. He was pondering the events ahead.

Lester shifted in his seat. His head turned toward the window again and his eyes darted back and forth. He counted fast as the onslaught of limestone fence posts came and went: "One, two three, four..." But the little game was short lived and Lester's head fell back. He was exhausted again.

Maybe going to see Emily and his new grandson was a mistake. He lingered over the thought. He didn't know what kind of reception he would get from Emily; they had parted with harsh words. She just plain up and left him, married Roger and that was that.

After all, didn't I raise her, pay for her education and make sure she went to the finest schools to keep her away from boys? He scowled.

Lester was a bachelor when Emily arrived on his doorstep. The man had not a whit of experience in raising a child back then, much less a girl. He had been stern with her, but Lester never struck her. Instead, the punishment Lester doled out came in vicious tongue-lashings that always made the little girl cry and run off to her room.

Lester knew she would eventually leave, he had hoped it would be after his own death. At any rate, all he only wanted now was to be accepted by the mother of his new grandson.

Maybe the goodies in his traveling valise would go a long way in mollifying Emily's anger. She had always loved looking at his jewels and coins; once, Lester secretly watched her as she and primped in front of a mirror with a small diamond tiara. It had made him laugh when he probably should have become angry. Looking back, he was glad he didn't scowl at Emily as she pretended to be grown up.

Lester was determined not to make the same mistakes with his grandson, Daniel. Yes, he resolved to make this trip a successful one, if only his old bones would hold out.

Jennie Mae Bullock sat next to him, contented and quiet. Big plans were brewing inside the young woman's mind, for it was never at rest. She was so preoccupied; she never cared a lick about the stares coming from a few passengers. *Let them stare all they want,* Lester had told her.

His traveling with the tall, winsome Negro woman had stirred some racist comments and stares. Back at the loading platform, the conductor insisted that she ride in "the other car." Lester steadfastly held his ground: "Dog blasted!" he shouted at the suggestion. "She's my nurse and I'm an old man," not caring how that would be interpreted. "You mind your own business!"

There was no more trouble and the pair rode the rest of the trip without much further incident, despite some strange looks from some white passengers in the White's Only Car.

Lester pulled out the train schedule and noted that Abilene was only six hours away. They'd stop for the night and continue west to Wahoo the next morning.

*****

Larry Washburne, a copy editor at the Austin Times, tore open the brown envelope with Holmes' story tucked inside. He sighed,

106

adjusted his glasses and started reading:

"A secret society is responsible for at least two murders and perhaps more in the tiny town of Wahoo, Texas, according to experts investigating the case…"

The story, (if you could call it that) was pitiful. It was a miasma of half-truths, distortions and old-fashioned misquotes intended only to bolster the reporter's own ego. Even worse, the three horrible photographs Holmes sent included a downright lousy head shot of this Manstill character.

But, then, the next paragraph just beat all: "This society, which has run amuck in Texas in the last few years, has even touched the sons of important men in this state." Holmes clearly didn't have any solid murder evidence. He not only libeled the two rangers who were investigating the case, but he libeled Frank Manstill as well. Washburne lost count of the allusions to homosexual activities, starting with his "great and good friend" and "inseparable companion" references.

"It is felt in these quarters that a further investigation is warranted, perhaps to the highest state levels," the copy thundered and blundered along. "Today, many sons of famous Texans will slumber in fear for what the 'morrow may bring: an untold misery," The story at least ended with a flourish, Washburn admitted.

The whole thing was a Holmes specialty and a fiasco at the same time. Holmes was sent to Wahoo to get a good story (and a few pictures, as well) but instead had sent this unvarnished tripe on the train back to the Main Office.

There was no way the paper could run it. With that, Washburne sliced the bombastic missive from its original nine pages into two small, comparatively tame paragraphs:

Authorities are presently investigating two murders in the town of Wahoo, in Natches County. The Texas Rangers issued a statement acknowledging the deaths and report that 'an intense investigation is underway,' according to Lt. Marcus Cramer, lead investigator.

The town of 309 souls has not been the site of a murder since 1901,
according to Town Mayor Regis Green. One suspect has already been cleared,
he added.

The editor finished his addition to page 12 and dropped the page
into the pneumatic tube at the side of the desk. He watched as the
rolled-up paper slid through the tube to the desks of the morning
editors at the Austin Times.

As a final decision, no pictures ran alongside the final version of
Holmes' story. The two paragraphs, unchanged, ran in the June 6,
1926 evening edition under the State News banner. Some time on
the composing table in the press room before deadline, a
composing room editor inserted an ordinary advertisement next
to Holmes' butchered "story;" it was an advertisement for
Murphy's Solid Cow Dung, *"Guaranteed to Improve Your Crop Yield."*

******

CHAPTER EIGHTEEN:
SUSPICIOUS MINDS

The Deacons stood on the dusty platform as they waited for Lester's train to arrive at the Wahoo station. Emily glanced at Daniel, who lay sleeping in his wooden homemade pram, blissfully unconcerned as usual. *If only I could be so calm,* she thought.

Emily had bitten her nails almost to the quick over the last two days in varying degrees of anticipation and fear of Lester's imminent arrival; Roger had scolded her over resuming an annoying childhood habit.

"I don't care," she answered. "This is making me crazy. When he finds out about the jewels and the money, he'll get angry and I'll be in a lot of trouble. Oh, Roger… if he doesn't know, do we have to tell him?" she pleaded.

He didn't relent, however strong her words. Roger was sure Lester would not punish Emily if they just told the truth. Finally, she reluctantly agreed, but she managed to get one concession from Roger; he would talk to Lester the day after he arrived and not just after arriving in Wahoo.

Roger agreed but if the truth be told, was also nervous about performing this chore. His last memory of the old man was of a wraith-like figure swearing at the eloping pair as they walked out of his mansion in Oak Park for the last time.

"You'll be sorry!" he blustered at them like the hammer of the gods. "Don't come back and don't expect anything in my will, either!" he cruelly added.

Now, Lester was due to arrive any moment; neither Emily nor Roger was absolutely sure how Lester would behave. "What time does the schedule say it should be here?" Emily asked.

"About ten minutes ago," Roger dryly replied. Like his nervous wife he was not entirely looking forward to this meeting, either.

As he spoke, the rumbling of the train could be heard to the north. The tell-tale plume of black smoke slowly made its way south to the station. A few moments later the train pulled in and loudly screeched to a halt. Daniel never stirred, Emily noticed.

Emily saw a tall black woman depart the train at the First Class section and immediately turn to assist someone following her down the stairs. It was her uncle Lester. Her breath caught in her throat but she swallowed her fear and wheeled the pram towards him with Roger in quick pursuit. "Uncle Lester!" she cried.

Even through the thinning crowd, Lester looked every inch the traveling dandy in his white suit and matching white Panama hat. He peered in Emily's direction, smiled and waved. "Emily!" She noticed he looked pale but otherwise healthy.

"You are looking well, Emily," Lester amiably said as Emily reached him with Roger a step behind. He turned and looked at him. "Roger." He offered his hand. "Congratulations."

"Glad to see you, Lester," Roger said through half-gritted teeth.

So far, so good, Emily thought.

"Meet Daniel, your grandson," Emily cooed to her relative. Lester looked down at the baby carriage at his sleeping grandson and beamed.

"Oh, my..." his voice seemed to crack for a moment and he stared at the dozing creature that was his grandson. "He looks like a Taylor," he announced with a grin. "Is he well?"

Emily laughed. "Uncle, he sleeps like the baby he is. He's a perfect sleeper. In fact, that baby sleeps more than he is awake. Not that we are complaining, of course."

"Outstanding. Oh, excuse me, Roger, Emily: may I introduce Jennie Mae Bullock, my nurse?" Lester turned to the woman who towered over her patient by four inches.

Jennie Mae did not offer her hand but nodded in Roger and Emily's direction. "May I see the baby?" she asked.

"Of course," Emily replied. She pulled back the small dust curtain and let Jennie Mae lean over and peeked at Daniel. "My. He is a big one," she remarked. "He has big hands, too."

"He should. He was almost nine full pounds," Emily answered. "He takes after his daddy," she demurely added with a wink at Roger.

"Well. Lead on, Emily. Where am I staying?" Lester asked as the last of his bags were unloaded by the porter. Jennie Mae discreetly tipped the young man two dollars.

"I arranged for two private rooms in a very nice boarding house, Lester. Our local hotel is not the best."

"Excellent." Lester turned to Roger and smiled. "I trust you are taking good care of my niece and my grandson?"

"Yes sir."

"Grand. What are you doing for a living out here?" Lester queried Roger as he surveyed the semi-desolate, Texas plains. In back of the two men, Jennie Mae and Emily followed and talked about Daniel.

"I'm the second foreman at the Brick Factory. It's a very good job and we're doing pretty well," Roger answered. "After you get settled, we'll have you over the house for dinner.

"A house? Already? Very good, Roger. I'm impressed." Lester

111

lowered his voice. "I have a surprise for you and Emily; I think you will find it very interesting," Lester said conspiratorially.

Roger did not answer at first. He wondered what had changed the man he knew just a few short months before. Lester seemed amiable enough and not in a permanent rage over some implied slight; in fact, he seemed almost too nice so far. "I'm sure I will, Lester. How was the trip down here?"

"I forgot how long it takes to get somewhere nowadays," Lester admitted. "But, the train was on time for the most part and there were no serious problems. Overall, it was a good journey but Roger, this is the high point, seeing you and Emily and of course, little Daniel."

"How long are you staying, Lester?"

"Oh, as long as I feel like it, Roger. I'm in no hurry."

*****

Across town, the meeting between the two detectives and the mayor was not going as smoothly as Lester's arrival in Wahoo. In fact, the mayor sat in his office with his arms crossed and an intensely stubborn look on his face as he listened to Tillman explain what the findings were so far.

"In fact, mayor, we have heard some things about your son as well," Tillman said.

Green's face went ashen, a fact both men noticed. "What things?"

"Oh, there is a possibility he was involved…"

"Not in murder! He wasn't here when this happened!"

"No sir. I did not mean that," Tillman answered. "But he is in involved in some way, isn't he?" he probed.

"Absolutely not," Green replied.

112

"Mayor." Cramer stepped forward. "If there is anything you haven't told us, now is the time, sir. If we find out things later on our own, it will be harder on all those concerned."

Green knew the lawman wasn't bluffing. With his head in his hands, he told the sordid story of his son's indiscretion and immediate departure from Wahoo two years before, which validated what the other man had said to them in the barn.

The lawmen listened and glanced at each other during various parts of the mayor's testimony. It was exactly what their snitch Hayden had told them.

"So you knew Hamilton Daniels, then?" Tillman asked.

"Yes, I did. It was hard to not too around here." He scowled.

"Why did you lie to us in the beginning, then?" Cramer pressed.

"Because I knew you would draw the wrong conclusion," Green answered.

"Besides, that damn fool got killed because of something stupid he did, and my son had nothing to do with it," he defended.

"Do you have any idea who would kill Daniels, Mayor Green? Besides you?" Tillman stared at the mayor like a feral hunter sizing up a stumbling prey.

"No, I don't. I almost wish anyone else but Daniels had shown up dead," Green replied. He never blinked as he answered the question, a fact that was not lost on Cramer as he watched the interrogation.

"Tell us about the restaurant receipt, mayor. Why did you hide it from us?"

Green was genuinely surprised. "What paper?" He looked at the two detectives, plainly not understanding the question.

Tillman explained his discovery of the receipt as Green listened.

113

He shook his head in emphasis. "I never saw a piece of paper like that." He stared at Tillman, who just smiled slightly.

"Who was with you when the picture was taken? Besides your photographer, that is."

"Jack Welborn."

"I see. Can you look at this, mayor?" Tillman said as he slid the picture of Daniel's body on the table. The picture had Daniels on his right side. In the extreme corner were the tips of a pair of black boots. "Whose feet are these?"

"Welborn's. I don't have a pair like that," Green said. "I only wear brown boots or black shoes. I don't have a pair of black boots."

"Interesting."

Cramer knew his sergeant had made his point. The mayor had fingered Welborn as a suspect although he himself was obviously under serious suspicion. The noose was tightening around the mayor's neck as he sat with his eyes locked on the table in front of him.

At that moment, the door opened and Willie Green walked in, surprised at the two ranger's presence in his father's office. "Sorry if I am interrupting something, gentlemen, but I came by to see my father."

"Ah, Mr. Green. I'm glad you just happened by," Tillman replied sarcastically. "We were just going to come and see you, weren't we, *lootenant*?

"Absolutely. Now is as good as a time as any. We'll talk to him in our office," Cramer said as he slipped his cane in his hand to leave. "We'll talk again, mayor."

"Actually, this is not a good time for this," Willie hedged.

"Perhaps we could agree to meet tomorrow?"

"That's not necessary. We can pretty much wrap up this investigation today," Tillman smoothly answered. Willie glanced at his father for help.

"Do as they say, Willie." Even in the dimming afternoon light, Regis' face was clearly lined with worry. He stared helplessly as the two detectives left the office on either side of his son.

*****

CHAPTER NINETEEN:
LESTER'S SURPRISE

Lester did a little two-step waltz in front of the mirror as he adjusted his tie. His dashing crisp blue and white Seersucker suit stole the show in the sparsely furnished room at Mrs. Blackwell's boarding house.

The room was scrubbed clean, however, just like the tiny privy down the hall, and Lester was comforted by the plainness of it all. The dapper dancer's silent audience included a porcelain pitcher and matching wash bowl, a chair, a small desk and a quilted bed.

He tossed his things on the bed. He didn't pay attention to the large window facing east that would later allow a much-too-early morning sun to spill onto his pillow. Tomorrow would find him pulling the covers over his grey head, anyway, and happily continuing to sleep after digesting Emily's lavish meal.

Lester checked again for the special package. It was still over there, on the bed. He was proud of himself for keeping the largess a secret; Emily would be rendered speechless by the gifts and the change in her old tormentor's ways.

Lester's thoughts drifted to Daniel sleeping in the carriage. He was still getting used to the idea of being a great uncle. A lifelong bachelor, he only recently discovered the soft spot he carried in his heart for children. This special, newfound fondness for the youngster whom he had met only once was overwhelming.

He was delighted, too, at the turn of events. The couple's reception had been warm; there was no trace of tension between Emily and him. Maybe he'll have a chance to be the uncle he wanted to be.

Jolted by the knock at the door, Lester called out: "Yes?"

"Mr. Taylor. It's about time to go," said Jennie Mae. He hoped her room had been as pleasant as his.

"I'll be right out." Lester took a last look in the mirror and pitched a scrap of hair across his forehead. He picked up the package, threw his cane over one arm and swung open the door.

Jennie Mae looked stunning in a fashionably tailored blue dress that fit her figure perfectly. It was as if she was someone else; a ravishing beauty just standing there waiting to accompany him.

"What's the matter, Mr. Taylor?" she asked in a teasing voice. She was confident that she looked divine in the dress which had been expertly selected for the occasion. It was her husband's favorite.

"My, my—you look lovely tonight, Miss Jennie." he blustered, turning a little red in the face.

"Well, you paid for it, sir," she said, as if to thwart the embarrassing moment for the both of them. Just then, two hotel guests passed them in the narrow hallway, and upon over-hearing her comment, they turned and stared.

Lester sported his first mean look of the day and glared back at them. He turned to Jennie Mae Bullock and said aloud: "Very well, nurse. Let's go. I'm hungry." Along the way, only a few Wahoo-ians took second looks at them. Lester was unfazed; his perfectly erect posture and jutting jaw seemed to beg for a sour comment from anyone.

"Evening, folks," Roger said when they stepped onto the porch of the little house. Emily stood at Roger's side with her hands at her sides.

Lester looked around the inside of the house with an air of a connoisseur. "This looks very nice," he remarked. Do you still have the divan sofa? My old bones are already a little tired."

"Absolutely. It cost an arm and a leg to get it here," Roger answered. "Come on in." He led them inside to the makeshift dining room. Emily's table had been set with their best china. Both Lester and Jennie Mae noted the oversized candelabra placed in the center. The awkward arrangement was all but forgotten when they turned and saw Daniel. He lay freshly fed and lay contentedly in his crib next to Lester's chair. His little eyes fluttered in a half-sleep.

"Well, *he* certainly looks happy," Lester remarked, laughing.

"And so will you when you see this meal, Uncle Lester," Emily said. Over the next hour, they dined and chattered over expertly prepared steak, potatoes, cornbread and black-eyed peas, a favorite of Lester's. The conversation remained cordial and superficial and did not divert into family history, much to everyone's relief.

After the plates were put away, Emily poured everyone a cup of Souther Brother's coffee and served some homemade apple pie. Both Lester and Jennie Mae remarked about the coffee's rich, deep flavor. "My, this is the best," Lester commented. "I am impressed and stuffed."

No one knew what to say during the coffee sipping. And no one but Lester knew what was coming when he made his announcement: "Folks," he said, glancing sideways to include Jennie Mae. "This is an important occasion."

Emily's hands slowly rose up and cupped her mouth. She looked wide-eyed at Roger, who was thinking the same thing. What could this be...? They both held their breath.

When Lester whipped out the special package from under his coat and held it up for everyone to see, Emily and Roger let out sighs of surprise loud enough that was heard by all. The old man delicately plucked away the layers of wrapping. Out came a pair of delicately handcrafted golden earrings which Lester held up in the light. Each was formed into the image of an eagle. Rows of tiny rubies lay twinkling across their moving wings.

"This fine jewelry came from the gold bazaars of Zanzibar, he boasted. He stepped toward Emily and deposited the two birds into her cupped hands.

"Do you remember them?" he asked. "You loved to play dress-up with these earrings."

"Oh, yes. I do," Emily said, surprised. "It was so long ago, Uncle Lester."

"Well, now they are yours, Emily," he dartingly interrupted. "And they're worth at least a thousand dollars in today's market."

He opened his valise, removed an envelope and rambled on about his remarkable journey. He told about a notable battle fought in Zanzibar that took place almost 30 years earlier. His acquaintance, the Sultan Hamid bin Thuwaini, had died on August 25, 1896. Two hours after the sultan's death, a usurper broke into the Palace and declared himself as its ruler, Lester explained.

"You can imagine what a remarkable show of Victorian gunboat diplomacy it was that the Royal Navy was summoned to evict the villian," Lester commented, thinking they would understand the meaning behind such a momentous occasion.

"Two days later, on August 27, at precisely 9 o' clock, three warships opened fire. Within 45 minutes, they reduced the Palace to rubble and killed the usurper," he told. "The bombardment is still known as the 'Shortest War in History'."

Everyone in the room gasped, including Jennie Mae. They could not imagine having known a sultan.

"Roger, there are twenty-five gold coins inside this envelope. They're worth two thousand dollars. I know you will use the money wisely for Daniel," he said softly.

Stunned with the outrageous presentation so far, Roger and Emily stared at each other over this man who had nearly run over

119

them and then out of town and threatened Emily with disinheritance.

"Roger, I also have a thousand dollars in cash for you. It's for you," he emphasized again, "As the man of this warm, wonderful house. It was the dowry I never paid—with interest." He handed a flummoxed Roger a bank check. "Oh, there is something else here," he continued. "It's a matter of my will…"

Emily peered over her shoulder at Jennie Mae. The nurse couldn't have known about this, Emily thought. And she hadn't made any gestures to give the family privacy, either. The three remained seated in front of the odd candelabra on the table. Lester continued, "I have a copy of it here for you, Emily, straight from my lawyer in Chicago. It's authentic, Emily. It bears a valid registration number, right here." he pointed to the page.

"You don't have to read it now, but let's just say, you both will be well-taken care of, and so will Daniel," he added.

Emily's soft voice broke the silence.

"Uncle Lester, this is so wonderful. You know I never hated you, I just felt sad about how lonesome you were," Emily confided. Lester stared straight down into his lap. He must have seemed pathetic to them, he thought. He didn't look up for the longest time.

"I know, child," he said. He raised his head. His eyes were soft now and not at all as she had remembered them. "I wasn't a good influence on you. But, thanks to Jennie Mae, I feel like a new man. I had debts to pay and this was one of them."

Emily and Roger's eyes moved to the prim Negro woman who had prompted Lester's change. Lester interrupted their stares: "Well, I ain't gettin' any younger and they always say, 'You can't take it with you,' so that's why I came here," he concluded. He sat up straight and folded his hands in front of him.

Emily needed a gesture from Roger; some sign that would help guide her thinking. One thing was certain: she knew her husband would never divulge the stolen jewels and money after this. Roger grinned with a twinkle in his brown eyes.

Emily rose, moved over to the rail-thin man who had caused her so much pain over the years and hugged him. They were both shaking. However, her tremors were prompted by the realization she still had her freedom. And it was up to her to keep it that way.

******

Willie Harden Green's dinner was hardly a celebration. After leaving his father's office, the two Texas Rangers left him to sit alone in a spare room while they conferred next door. To Willie, a trained lawyer, those few minutes were Hell on earth. His heart beat wildly through his shirt and he started to sweat. Worse, his leg jiggled up and down like an engine piston underneath the table.

He resisted the urge to bite his fingernails by holding his hands firmly in his lap. Willie had learned some techniques in masking nervousness. That knowledge from his law classes came in handy. But that was an exercise; this was real. Being questioned by these rangers was not like any college exercise.

The questions swirled around in his mind: *What did he know about two years ago and Hamilton Daniel's extortion attempt? Most of all, what did the detectives know and why did his father look so worried?*

Willie decided the situation was beyond his control. He considered denying everything and leaving town. That had worked before. But, now he'd have to get past these two lawmen.

Finally, the door opened and the short detective walked in. Without making eye contact, he pulled up a chair. Willie noticed that in his right hand was a sheath of papers in a folder. Thumbing through the file, Tillman stopped on a particular page and looked over the table at Willie.

His eyes were intense and hawk-like which made Willie's insides turn into liquid jelly.

"Mr. Green, I am Sergeant Louis Tillman, Texas Rangers. You can call me officer, Ranger Tillman, or sir. "He smoothed the page and looked down. "Tell me what you know about Hamilton Daniels."

Willie summoned an unexpected calm. He explained the events that took place two years ago, leaving out the raw details. The lawman's mask of dispassion barely moved. Tillman had learned that a guilty man's own words usually hung himself eventually, so why not let him talk away?

As he spoke, Willie felt a trickle of sweat nibble its way along his cheek.

"Where were you on May 1ˢᵗ, 1926?" Tillman asked.

"I was still in New Haven, officer. You know that." A hint of smugness flickered across his face. This was safe territory.

"I know. When did you last see Daniels?"

"I last saw him alive, two years ago," Willie affirmed.

Tillman thought it strange that Willie used the word "alive," but he continued: "Was Jack Welborn involved, then, with your..." he paused for the right word, "*disagreement* with Mr. Daniels?"

"Yes. He kept my father from bashing his head in. It's no secret," Willie huffed back.

"Whose head?"

"Franklin Hayden's. He was a friend of Daniels'. Hayden tried to extort money from my father."

"Did Daniels ever write you any letters?" Tillman asked, shifting his tactics.

"No. Not that I know of, sir."

"Never?"

"Never."

"That's strange. I was under the real impression there was a lengthy correspondence between you two. At least, that's what the letters say." Tillman wrenched forward in his seat and glared hard at Willie.

"What letters are you talking about? I have no such letters. This is a farce," he shrilled at Tillman.

"We'll see what a farce it is when we get the letters analyzed by the FBI's experts, Mr. Green. I can promise you that. It's just a matter of time. I thought you might want to spare us the same time and tell us about the letters first."

In fact, there were no letters. This effective diversionary tactic had a devastating effect on Willie Green. He wiped his dewy face with a handkerchief. The door opened and the taller lawman appeared, also carrying a sheath of papers and an ebony cane.

"We looked into your story and it checks out," Lieutenant Cramer said. "You were not here when Daniels was murdered. That is true." Referring to the documents, Cramer nodded at Tillman, who nodded back.

"Mr. Green, we will continue this talk tomorrow. I assume you are here to stay in Wahoo." Cramer noted.

"Yes. I'm sure you've heard that I'm taking over my father's factory."

"Good. Then, enjoy your dinner. We are finished here, for now," Cramer replied.

"Well, good evening, gentlemen." Willie's unsteady legs revealed a shaken young man. He couldn't believe the whole episode was over—if only just for one night.

Cramer waited until the door closed and he smiled at Tillman.

"I don't think he did it, but I think he hired someone to who did."

"I agree, sir. The mayor knows a lot more than he's telling us."

"And so does Welborn. Let's question put the pressure on him and then we'll see what comes out."

*****

CHAPTER TWENTY:
HEADLINE GAMES

Inside his room at the Ram's Inn, Wesley Oliver Holmes III lay half-dressed on the bed with a faraway look in his eyes. The hand-rolled marijuana cigarette he was holding created a grayish haze that hovered over the bed for more than an hour.

After filing his three-column opus, Holmes spent the remainder of the day wandering through Wahoo. It took about ten minutes. He registered the sights and sounds, and made mental notes for the upcoming bestseller he envisioned: "Murder in Wahoo." Wesley saw the murder as more of an opportunity than anything.

For certain, the dead homosexual and the other dead men were inconsequential to him. But the book it would spur could escalate his career. It could make him as famous as F. Scott Fitzgerald, he thought. At least fame would put him a better position to find his own Zelda and live the good life.

Sipping wine in a Parisian café surrounded by brilliant bohemian writers was a far cry from roasting in this Texas hot house. Until now, his only other option was to slave away in a dreary newspaper office, a wasted talent, waiting for someone to die to get promoted.

But there was still one hitch in his hazy thinking. In spite of his numerous interviews with locals, Holmes was still not sure who had killed Hamilton Daniels. But then again, it really didn't matter *who* killed Daniels; the real news was *why*. If only he could answer that, his plan to present the scandal to the world in his own literary style and let the riches roll in…

"Mr. Holmes. Delivery!"

He shook his head and returned to reality. Opening the door, he looked down upon another of Wahoo's endless supply of street urchins. The lad handed over a small bundle wrapped in string. The grey fog wafted out from the room and made the kid's nose wrinkle as he tried to scurry away. .

"Not so fast," the journalist scolded. He fished out a dollar bill. "Thank you," Holmes told him with an air of authority. The kid snatched the money and skipped away.

Holmes collapsed on the bed again. With shaking hands, he opened the package and a copy of that day's Austin Times popped out. He closed his eyes, took a deep breath and suddenly coughed hard again. He started to read.

The top story on the front page was about the mysterious disappearance of Aimee Semple McPherson, the founder of the International Church of the Foursquare Gospel. She vanished on May 18 in Los Angeles. Almost a month later, it was assumed she had drowned; now she had been seen by credibly witnesses in New York City.

He cursed his bad luck. Yeah, the story of the missing evangelist was of far more important than his own. He even had a bet with the boys in the newspaper's back room that the missing woman, a noted publicity hound, had probably staged her own disappearance in order to bolster her radio audience.

He scanned the front page again. It was full of other news items happening around the globe and in Texas but there was no mention of Wahoo, or the murders at all. And none of his photographs were there! Wesley was puzzled and perplexed.

Then he rifled through the pages. After reaching page five, he knew something had gone terribly wrong. He almost threw the whole thing aside in disgust when he finally spotted the diminutive mention hidden under "Texas News."

Was this his article? Holmes couldn't believe his eyes; it had been reduced to two lousy paragraphs written by someone else. He swallowed hard, coughed again and looked at it closely. He had to suffer through the terrible story, (if one could call it that) four times before spotting an envelope that had been tucked inside. It had his name on it.

Holmes unfolded the paper and read it out loud. It was from his publisher and Austin Times' owner, Chester Gregg:

"Dear Mr. Holmes: Your services at this paper are no longer required. Contact the payroll department for delivery of your last paycheck. Good luck in the future."

The stunned journalist didn't know that his timing for covering the story couldn't have been worse. In his zeal to get a scoop, the journalist did not know one important detail that spurred Gregg's fury: The publisher's youngest son had also been compromised by the Flamingo Club two months earlier. At that time, the extortionists demanded and got substantial payment through an intermediary. And, not surprisingly, the scandal never surfaced.

Now, with his incomplete and misguided attempt at stardom, Wesley Oliver Holmes III was anything but a newspaper superstar. And his career at the Austin Times was over.

******

The detectives met Franklin C. Hayden at the usual interrogation spot in the town barn late at night. They noticed he seemed to be more furtive than usual. While Cramer spoke to the "fag rat," as he called him, Tillman guarded the doors.

"I have something else for you," Hayden said. "I heard Regis Green was furious when Daniels showed up here a few days before his son was expected to arrive. He and the sheriff arranged to get Daniels out of town. He didn't have a choice."

"Well, that arrangement didn't work because Daniels ended up here," Cramer answered.

"Yeah." Hayden said. "The sheriff ordered his deputies to get Hamilton's personal belongings after he died." Hayden smiled at this news. "But they forgot these; I found 'em hidden under Ham's bed."

He handed a satchel to Cramer. "What's in here?" Cramer asked.

"Nothing much, really," he reported. "A diary and some papers—I didn't read them, though. The sheriff has the rest."

Tillman emerged from the darkness. "When did the sheriff get Daniels' items?" he asked.

"The same day Hamilton died. That's what that disgusting man at the hotel said," Hayden replied.

"Who was that, Jellison Briscoe?"

"Yes. That's what he told me."

"Briscoe never told us anything like that," Cramer said, under his breath.

Tillman nodded in agreement.

"Well, that's all I have for you. I'm taking Ham's body back to Austin by train tomorrow. I did all I could. I hope you'll find the bastards."

The Texas Rangers knew they were sitting on a powder keg of new and interesting information. Taking no chances, they scurried back to their makeshift office. They were glad to end the meeting before passers-by could catch the lights blazing inside while they pored over the dead man's things.

*****

"Roger. Are you awake?" Emily whispered.

"Yeah. I guess I am, *now*."

"We have to talk."

"Not now, Emily. I have to work in the morning." He rolled over and yanked at the quilted cover. It didn't budge.

"No, you don't. It's Saturday, remember? Or did you forget your promise?" she retorted.

In fact, in the excitement of Lester coming into town, Roger had completely forgotten to ask his boss for Saturday off. But he knew this wasn't the real point of this discussion.

He sighed and gave in. "I didn't forget. Okay, I have tomorrow off," he resigned. "Happy?" Roger made a mental note to have the third plant assistant foreman, Perry Haskell, come in and oversee the Brickhouse operations until the plant shut down for the weekend.

"Good," she purred. "I wanted to talk about something else, though."

"Fancy that. We already talked about getting a car, Emily. We don't need one."

"This has nothing to do with a car," she pouted. "I have a plan, Roger. Hear me out, all right?"

"A plan for what?" Roger was stone awake now. He wanted to remind that it was her last plan that had gotten them stuck in the first place.

"You know…*the stuff*," she whispered.

"We already agreed about the stuff, Emily."

"Listen. If I could get everything back to Oak Park without Lester realizing it, then we wouldn't have to tell him, would we? We'd get them anyway in his will, so there was no need to have stolen them in the first place," she reasoned.

"That makes sense." Roger was intrigued now. Maybe she had actually come up with a better chance to save face. He decided to listen.

129

"He's been wonderful to us. I feel so badly that I took it now, but at the time…" her voice ended with a sigh of desperation which pulled at Roger's heart strings. "Well, how could I have known?"

"You couldn't have known, Emily. There's a case here for never stealing under any circumstances, but we're beyond that.

"How are you going to get it back to Oak Park?"

"Let me work on it. If I fail, we'll just have to pay him a visit. The main thing is, Lester can never, ever find out. Did you look at the copy of the will?"

"Yes. Everything is split four ways between you, the cousin you have never seen, Daniel and a foundation in Lester's name. The sum is unbelievable," Roger admitted.

"Follow my instincts, Roger, unless you want to risk losing the money" she hissed.

"Okay, Emily. But if this gets out of hand, I'm taking over."

"So let me try, at least," she pleaded.

"I don't like this. I think there is a better way," he countered.

"Really? Well, let me tell you mister, I have seen his moods. He's in a good one for a change. And, for whatever reason, Lester has become a 'new man.' I don't know how, but I feel it has something to do with that new nurse of his. I'd put even money on it."

"Go on."

"I'm going to enlist her help. She's our only hope, Roger. No one but Jennie Mae can get within a hundred feet of Lester's study where he keeps all his treasures. I know that as well as anyone."

"You mean, ask her to secretly return the stuff to his safe? Do you think she'd do that for us? Can we trust Jennie Mae to really

130

stay quiet about the whole thing?"

"I don't know. I only hope she has compassion for us. She seems to be a good soul and look what she's done for Lester," she observed. "I noticed his eyes are clearer and he has a lot more energy. I remember he said as much at dinner. In fact, he even ate a full meal. I don't think I've ever seen him do that."

"Good for him." His eyes rolled and annoyance oozed with every syllable.

"All I'm asking for is a chance, Roger," Emily begged. "Can you give your wife at least that?"

Roger wished he had simply gone to sleep.

"It's fine by me. See what you can do with the nurse, but if it comes down to it, I *will* tell Lester. And that is a promise I *will* keep, Emily. Goodnight."

*****

CHAPTER TWENTY ONE:
THE ROPE TIGHTENS

"Wake up, Briscoe."

The dozing man was jarred awake by Lieutenant Cramer's harsh voice. He opened his eyes and saw the officer standing there ready to poke him with his cane. "I have some questions for you."

"Do I have to?" He sat up and squinted.

"Tell me this, when Daniels was in town, where did he stay?"

"Here, mostly—when he *was* in town. He traveled a lot, you know," Briscoe snickered.

Cramer ignored the implication. "Which room?"

For some reason, he liked Room 6, I believe. Do you want to see it?"

"Not at the moment. Who visited Daniels' room either before or after he died?"

"One fella named Hayden, I remember."

"No one else?"

"No." Briscoe's eyes blinked fast. He was awake now and couldn't understand where this was going. The room had been cleaned many times since then. What could they find there?

"Really? Not Sheriff Woodward or any other deputy?"

"Oh, yeah, sure. That's right," he said. "Them, too."

"I get the impression you aren't being too honest with me, there Mister Jellison. Let's say we put you in lockup for a day and see if your memory improves. And then we can talk in private." Cramer had the look of a man who would not wait for that to happen.

"No, we don't need to do that. I hate jails. The food is lousy."

"Good. Then let's get smart about this. When did these people visit? After Daniels died?"

"Yessir. Except that Hayden fella. He came a coupla days later," Briscoe answered.

"No one else?"

"No. That I *would* know."

"Well, that's an improvement, Jellison," Cramer responded mockingly. "Now we're getting somewhere and you get to stay put. Now, show me Daniels' old room."

******

While Lieutenant Cramer questioned Briscoe, Tillman had Jack Welborn squarely in his interrogative sights. At first, Welborn was glad to see the burly sergeant instead of his boss; he was convinced Cramer was a maniac with a badge.

Tillman looked at Welborn. "So, Jack. You were there when they found the body, right?"

"Roger Deacon was there, too," Welborn offered but caught himself after it was too late. Mentioning Deacon made him appear too eager to deflect responsibility. Welborn made a mental note to be more careful.

"Correct. But we are talking about *you*, not *him*."

133

Welborn sat back. This time he said nothing.

"I'll take that as a yes. Well, here's the problem. We're looking for some missing evidence. And we have proof, Jack. Would you happen to know anything about that?"

"Like what?

"Like anything, Welborn. Don't play with me."

At that moment, Welborn forgot about the psycho lieutenant; Tillman's body leaned forward in his chair and his face was only a few inches from his. Intimidated and scared, he moved back slowly.

"Sheriff Woodward has it. He took it with him and that's the truth. I never took anything; I just looked at the body and saw who it was. I can't say it surprised me that it all happened, seeing how Daniels carried on around here."

The statement confirmed Tillman's hunch. Woodward had a larger role in this from the beginning. Not mentioning the evidence was damning. "What else did Woodard do?"

"He told me to keep my mouth shut and not let the word out about Daniels'—uh, you know. No one figured Green would call you Texas Rangers in here, I reckon."

Tillman jotted some notes. "Were you at the murder scene?" the sergeant asked. He wanted to catch Welborn off guard.

"No-o. I wasn't," Welborn answered with a new and unexpected feeling of respect for the sergeant. He had more than underestimated Tillman's expert observation skills.

"So you weren't there at all?"

"I was at home."

"That's interesting, because here is a riddle: your boots are seen in this picture as well as a piece of paper that you said the sheriff took. Yet, other photos show *two* sets of those same boot prints leading up to the body, Welborn. Each set comes from a different direction. Now, how can that happen?"

"I don't understand."

"You said you walked up and saw Daniels' body. That would be one set of prints. Yet, the same kind of boot prints appear leading up to the body from an entirely different direction. The photograph doesn't lie."

Welborn frantically searched his brain for a way out. "Wait. I walked over to where Deacon was puking his lunch all over the sagebrush," he countered. "That explains that."

The sergeant grinned. "No, it doesn't, Jack. I spoke to Deacon. He said he walked away from Daniels body, not toward it. And I believe him because people rarely walk *into* something unpleasant, they walk *away from it*. And, the boot tracks—*your tracks*— coming from the other side of Daniels' body were not nearly as fresh."

Welborn didn't dare answer.

"Well, Jack, I think we can talk a lot better at the local jail here. I also think you and I need talk to Sheriff Woodward. Like right now."

"Am I under arrest?"

"Not at the moment. But I'll answer that after we see the sheriff. Let's go."

The two men walked out into the overcast afternoon towards the Wahoo jail; Tillman had the measured gait of a man in charge while Welborn loped behind with his head down.

Along the way, the two Texas Rangers spotted each other. It only took them a few minutes to confirm their need to see Woodward next.

Outside the jail, a deputy sat on a three-legged stool, whittling a piece of wood. "Howdy," he said. He didn't make a motion to stand.

"Is the sheriff here?" Cramer asked the recalcitrant lawman.

"Nope. He's in Abilene. Be back tomorrah, I guess."

"Who's in charge when he's gone?"

"The Mayor, I guess. It sure ain't me."

"Thank goodness for small favors," Cramer replied.

"Huh?"

"Have him come see me the minute he gets back," he snapped.

"We'd be much obliged," Tillman added, stepping forward. "It's important."

"Okay. I'll do that." The laconic deputy continued whittling, oblivious to almost everything else.

"Come on, *lootenant*," Tillman interjected before his boss could lose his temper. "We'll see the sheriff when he gets back. I have an idea. I think we can let Mr. Welborn go. He's not going anywhere until tomorrow, right, Jack?"

"No. I have to work at the quarry."

Cramer sensed that the sergeant was burning to tell him something but not in Welborn's presence. "Fine. We'll see you tomorrow, Jack. Count on it."

The relieved man thanked the lawmen and scurried away as fast as he could.

"Louis, I think this idea of yours is going to get us closer to getting on a train and going home," Cramer quipped. "Tell me I'm wrong."

"You are rarely wrong, sir. Let's go back to the office; I want you to hear me out. I'll need your approval for this plan to work."

******

Holmes stared down at the few dollars he had counted out on the thin bedspread. Forty dollars and some change. It was all he had left and his final paycheck was back in Austin. The train back would cost ten, so he actually only had enough to stay in Wahoo for a day—two at best—before he'd be stuck there, dead broke.

Here was another Grand Canyon of circumstances. A huge story was unraveling before him and now he was a reporter without a newspaper affiliation. But almost in the same moment, Holmes came up with a solution. He'd have to find the murderer himself. Then he'd go back to Austin and give them a story they would *have* to publish.

He looked over some of his notes. *Let's see*, he mused. *I've covered Manstill's involvement...*Then Holmes recalled something. He got out a small stack of notebooks and, starting with the one on top, began thumbing through the pages. *Where was that?*

He remembered a small item, a note that he'd written in haste: the hotel clerk had casually mentioned something about Room 6. Finally, his finger ran across an illegible scribbling that ran into the margin. Holmes turned the second little book on its side and squinted at his own handwriting. The hotel clerk said that Room 6 had been Hamilton Daniels' favorite.

After dressing for dinner, he headed downstairs to the lobby desk. There was Jellison Briscoe in his usual spot. Approaching the desk under the auspices of discussing his bill, he spotted the key to Room 6 (and his future) dangling there, directly behind the surly-faced man.

"That'll be twelve dollars for two more days," Briscoe said with his hand already outstretched.

"For that tiny room? It doesn't even have a toilet," Holmes sniffed.

137

Briscoe was baffled. "You didn't say anything before, mister. You want a toilet? Room 6 has one," he countered. "That'll be fourteen dollars for two days."

"You have a deal. I will move my things immediately after I come back from dinner," Holmes said. He laid down part of his dwindling money and took the key to Room 6.

Briscoe grunted as he slammed the cash drawer shut and slithered back into his overstuffed chair.

That evening, Holmes enjoyed what was probably was of his last dinners at Souther's Restaurant. At least it was a fine one of beef stew, cornbread and of course, coffee. Afterward, he anxiously returned to his room and started moving his things down the hall, dropping them in front of door number 6.

He unlocked it and stepped inside, proud that he'd come up with this idea so quickly. In fact, the room was an upgrade with a private toilet and a larger basin. There in the entryway he brushed by the basin, a beguiling specimen of a vessel that was mounted on a plaster column with scrolled corners. Holmes lacked the architectural vocabulary to describe the thing.

He thought it resembled a Romanesque baptismal font or a replica of Solomon's basin in the Temple at Jerusalem. Regardless, he was certain he was facing a shrine to the wash gods.

As he pushed his bags inside, one snagged the pedestal and made it wobble. He snared the basin before it could tumble to the floor.

While putting it back into place, he noticed something in the column's plaster surface. With some careful prodding, a small hole came into view. He pulled a piece of wire from his valise and poked it inside. Hollow. As he brought the wire back out, it pulled open a small door to a well-concealed vault. Holmes was not surprised at this hideaway. He and other travelers often used their imaginations to find places to conceal their alcohol or valuables. There was even a name for this novelty: The Hootch Hidey-Hole.

What surprised him was what he found: sheets of paper folded tightly and bound with a red ribbon. He carefully fished them out and opened one. His wide-open eyes traveled downward to Hamilton Daniels' signature. It was a letter the dead man had once penned to someone identified only as "U-U."

"Bingo!" he said out loud. "Love letters!"

But who was this U-U? The code name triggered Holmes mental backtracking for a few minutes. Well for now, he thought, one thing was certain: these letters furnished proof that whoever "U-U" was, he had been in Wahoo the week that Daniels was killed.

Wesley Oliver Holmes III could barely contain himself. Luck was finally turning in his favor. Maybe he'd find the murderer just in time, before his money ran out. He stretched out on the bed and reached for the marijuana box. This story would break all records. He'd happily give the Austin Times first crack at it. And he'd love to have the publisher Desmond Glenn pay dearly to get it.

*****

CHAPTER TWENTY TWO:
NEGOTIATIONS

Trying her best, Emily steeled her nerves to put her plan into place. Without the black nurse's help, she would be exposed and there would be Hell to pay from her uncle Lester.

After their dinner the previous evening, Emily took Jennie Mae Bullock aside and invited her to lunch. "We should get to know each other," she said. Jennie Mae was pleasantly surprised. "That would be lovely, Emily. I can fill you in on how your uncle Lester has come to change over the last year."

The next day at Souther's, Emily ruminated again about her desperate scheme and wondering if it would work; there was no alternative to getting the jewels and money back into Lester's mansion without him knowing it. Just how she was going to present it all to Jennie Mae had yet to be determined. The entire thing deprived her of much needed sleep and caused unwanted dark circles to form under her eyes. *"I'll just hope and pray the words come out right,"* she thought.

Finally Jennie Mae entered the restaurant and a few Wahooians turned to look. The only three blacks in Wahoo worked at the Manstill Ranch and hardly ever came around. Oblivious to their stares, Jennie Mae gracefully breezed in looking charming and fresh in a handsome suit. She smiled at Emily and sat down.

"I'm glad you could make it, Mrs. Bullock," Emily said with her hands trembling under the table.

"You can call me Jennie Mae," she said. "I must tell you; this has been a worth-while trip. I've met Mr. Taylor's family and I know it has been a positive experience for him." They both picked up their menus. "I'm famished. You too?"

"I could eat half of Texas," Emily joked. "Where's Lester?"

"Well, I have no idea why, but he's talking to the mayor."

Emily wondered what kind of business her uncle would have with the mayor of Wahoo, but her thoughts shifted to her rumbling stomach.

Both ladies ordered the Souther Lunch Special: a half-plate of marinated beef ribs, a spicy cole slaw salad and chocolate dessert, all for two dollars.

While they waited to be served, Emily started the conversation by urging Jennie Mae to reveal some Oak Park gossip; Jennie Mae obliged gleefully. Her friends, she said, held long-term positions as nurses and house women for the stuffy denizens of Oak Park; and thanks to the invention of the telephone, the scuttlebutt spread quickly.

Jennie Mae's open and friendly manner put Emily at ease. Emily decided not to press her luck, but to wait for the after-dessert coffee to bring it up. Putting her thoughts to one side, she savored the spicy ribs and other treats.

Lunch seemed to stretch into hours. "That was a glorious meal, Emily. Now, a nice coffee like the kind we had last night would be perfect."

"There's a reason I asked you to lunch, Jennie Mae..." Emily decided to blurt it out.

"I know," she responded. "You are wondering who I am and why I suddenly appeared in your uncle's will."

Hiding her surprise, Emily answered, "That's true. But I already figured that out. Very few women have managed to stay with Uncle Lester for any length of time; he respects one who stands up to him, although like most men, he also hates the idea."

"I know. You should hear him talk about women voters."

141

Both women laughed because even though women had won the legal right to vote seven years earlier, many men still resented the ruling.

"I want to know one thing: Why was my uncle so kind to us? Is there something I should know?"

"Lester is a lonely man who was heavily addicted to morphine," Jennie Mae explained. "But, I have a secret for you: I did nothing except gradually give him lower doses; I also came up with some home remedies to help him sleep better without the drugs. Within a week, he changed dramatically; instead of lying in his room all day, he would do almost anything to get out of that old house."

This was a woman Emily could trust. "The *real* reason I asked you here is this: I feel certain that I can trust you to keep a secret. I need your help. The only thing I can offer in return is my gratitude—*for life*." Emily lowered her head, and placed her chin squarely in cupped hands. Looking up, she told the story about her parents' death and of being taken in by Lester. Jennie Mae nodded her head when she got to the part about the verbal abuse and Lester's extreme moods.

Jennie Mae listened attentively, without interruption. A contrite Emily dropped the big confession. Jennie Mae's eyes never blinked as Emily described taking the jewels and the money. "I want to give them back, Jennie Mae. But Lester can never, *ever* know. Will you help me?"

After what seemed like forever, Jennie Mae sat back in thought. Slowly she replied, "I will help you, but I want no money out of this; I will take everything back and hide them for you."

"You will? Oh, God bless you, Jennie Mae!" Emily rose from her chair and reached out to hug her. She started to cry, this time with joy. Roger would never believe the news.

"I don't blame you, Emily—I may have done the same thing— Lord knows I would have been tempted, the way your uncle acts sometimes. My first boss man was a lot like Lester; he pushed me around, he hit me, too. He was a scoundrel. And here's a secret for you, Emily: Before I left him to learn nursing with my cousin in Ohio, I did the same thing."

"You did? You were never caught?" Emily asked, incredulous.

"He was a drunk, but a rich one. He never noticed anything missing. For a long time afterwards, I felt guilty. But I just set my mind on other things."

Emily's instincts had been on target. Miraculously, the plan appeared as if it would work, she was sure of it. "Do you know when Lester wants to go back to Oak Park?"

"He told me to check the local train schedule for this Saturday," Jennie Mae answered.

"I feel so much better. I won't forget this," Emily vowed.

"Good. I may hold you to it. Now, let's finish our coffee so we can go back and see that beautiful boy of yours."

*****

Angel Rodriquez waited until nightfall to approach the Texas Rangers' office.

Since he stumbled across Crosby's body some days before, he kept his ears open for clues while working as a cook on the Manstill Ranch. Now he was ready to divulge some new facts to the lawmen, but he was afraid of being seen.

Tillman opened the door, surprised to see the nervous Mexican. Motioning him into the stuffy room, he cleared a seat and, speaking in Spanish, he asked Angel to take a chair. Cramer sat in the corner and listened.

"Senor, I told you, I see that man before. Well, I heer something yesterday," he started. "I heer the *vaqueros* talking and they say Crosby come to shoot at you to make you afraid and – *vamos*."

143

"Si. We know. But who paid Crosbie to come here?"

"I no know. But the *vaqueros* say they see my boss and Green talking out there in the mountains." He pointed to the north. "They were on horses."

"It was them? No mistake?"

Rodriquez smiled. "No mistake. Everyone know them."

Cramer sat up at the Mexican's statement. "When did this happen?"

"The same day you come here."

"Do you think Crosbie killed Hamilton Daniels?

"No. He leave us long before that," the young man answered with confidence. "He not a nice man. He call me 'La Cucaracha' and he spit on me. He no like my food some times when he drink too much *tequila*."

Tillman nodded, getting the picture. "Why did you come to us?"

"I thin' you want to know," he replied, confused by the question.

Cramer walked around the table and over to Rodriguez. "The Texas Rangers thank you," he said, producing a ten-dollar bill from his pocket. It was from a discretionary cash account the rangers used to help get valuable information. So far, he had paid out almost fifty dollars on this trip, a fact his boss would probably question.

"No. No. I no want *dinero*," Rodriguez said as he shook his head.

This was something new. Usually their sources would grab the money and make a quick exit. The two rangers wondered why Rodriquez didn't take the money.

Instead, he stood and nervously peered out the window. "I go now," he stated. "Is that ho-kay?"

144

"Yes. And thank you, again," Tillman said as he escorted him to the door. Rodriquez looked out and took another glance up and down the street before he disappeared into the shadows.

"Well. What an interesting development, Louis. Do you see Manstill and Green in cahoots?" Cramer asked.

"At first, I didn't. But now, I think they made a truce because of us. And it didn't work."

"No, it didn't. Okay, so let's hear the rest of your plan to catch these crooks so we can go back home," Cramer said. "My boss wants another report from me tomorrow morning and it ain't getting any earlier."

"Yes sir. As I said before, this mystery is falling into place. I know it is a gamble, but…"

At that moment, a loud knock interrupted their train of thought.

Tillman hollered, "Who is it?"

"Wesley Holmes."

Tillman turned and looked at his boss, who sighed and rolled his eyes. "Better let him in."

Holmes walked in and took a seat without an invitation. "I have something you would like to see," he huffed.

Cramer sat, impassive. "What do you have?"

"Some letters Daniels left behind in his room. I liberated them this afternoon." Holmes looked triumphant.

"All right, Holmes," Cramer said with a look on his face that said he was performing a disgusting task. "What do you want to know in return?"

"Nothing. I've been fired from my newspaper. I'm here as a private citizen, not a reporter."

"So you want money, then?"

"I want fifty dollars. No negotiation."

"Here's our offer: How does a night or two in jail sound for obstructing an investigation, Wesley?" Tillman thundered back. "It can be arranged, you know."

"That's not necessary. I'm offering you valuable information. You obviously have been handing out a lot of dough, from what I heard."

"How about this, Wesley: Thirty dollars and you get out of town and stay out, since you are here as a *private citizen*," Cramer retorted.

"I could do that," Holmes said with relief. He stuck his hand out at Cramer to shake on the deal; the lawman ignored the gesture.

"Good. So where are these letters?"

Holmes sat down again and handed a letter to Tillman. He gave the other to the Cramer who held it up next to what appeared to be another letter which he had obtained. It was written on the same pale paper.

Both detectives read this new information. Cramer put the letter down and actually smiled. "Good job, Wesley. I think this is worth fifty dollars." He took the money out of his pocket. "And when exactly will you leave Wahoo?"

"First train tomorrow morning," Holmes snapped. "I hate this town. I can't wait to leave."

"See to it that you do. And, since we paid for this information, I don't expect to see this in some newspaper article." Cramer said. "That would be illegal."

"Not unless it goes to trial, sir. Then it becomes public information. As I said before, I'm here as a private citizen. All I want is what anyone else would get for helping our fine lawmen," he said with bitter sarcasm.

Neither lawman really believed a word the slimy Holmes said, but getting him out of the way would be a bonus at this point in their investigation.

Cramer sought a confirming look from Tillman, who nodded back. "Good. Just so you understand that small point. Have a good trip back, Mr. Holmes."

******

CHAPTER TWENTY-THREE: ESCAPE

Frank Manstill recognized the loopy handwriting on the note from Sheriff Woodward's deputy. He'd seen Lieutenant Cramer's odd penmanship once before on a summons. Sure enough, he was being called to the jail, of all places, for a 3 o'clock meeting. The last word "Sharp" with a double underline agitated him as much as the meeting.

Hadn't he answered their questions? What could they want now? He slipped the note in his top pocket and mounted his horse to inspect his property. The timepiece on his saddle horn was creeping up on lunch time. One way or another, he decided, this fiasco with all its time-wasting inconveniences had better grind to an end.

******

Wesley Oliver Holmes III slumped down into his seat as the train pulled out of the Wahoo station. Thanks to the Texas Rangers, he now had enough money to get back to Austin, but his plans after that were an open sheet of paper. *Forget the glamorous future*, he thought. It had melted away the moment he was fired from the Austin Times.

And so much for pawning the fancy camera. They'd want that back before he could wrestle his final pay from his editor.

He was not entirely out of ideas, though. Maybe a book about the Texas Rangers would get him back into the arena. He could start right now by making notes about the case. He reached inside a pocket for a pencil. *Drat! No paper, either.*

Holmes was fooling himself, anyway. The big story had been his last chance to hit the top. He had time on a train ride to figure out how to salvage his career. But it was a long ride and he had some ideas.

I'm like a cat, he thought, *I've not yet run out of lives.*

******

As Holmes left Wahoo for good, Lester and Jennie Mae were awaiting their own permanent departure from the little town. They stood under umbrellas open against the searing sun on the station platform. Their bulging baggage was watched by a young porter.

Emily and Daniel were there to see them off, but Roger had to work. Emily saw Lester take Roger aside and hand him an envelope. She was dying to know what was in it. But, waiting was her forte – it had gotten through her early years with Lester.

Now Lester hugged her a dozen times. His affection continued to fill Emily with great joy. She never experienced even one embrace in Oak Park.

But Lester was clearly happy. He looked healthy. His skin was suntanned to a golden brown; it contrasted with his crisp white traveling suit. There was even a new addition to the ensemble: expensive brown and black rattlesnake-skin boots he found in a local store. Decades later they would be known as "cowboy boots" because of their distinctive style. However, no cowboy would ever really wear this fine footwear for a more practical reason – they were too good for the mud and dirt of the range.

Lester's mood was positively ebullient.

"You must come back to Oak Park," he told Emily.

"That would be wonderful, uncle." She stopped talking. The jubilance overshadowed everything and she was compelled to blurt out her awful secret. It was as if nothing, not even the worst discretion could come between her and her precious uncle now. Something welled up inside her and released a strong urge to let out the incriminating details and beg Roger for his forgiveness.

Then common sense took over.

Lester sensed the tension. "What's wrong, Emily?" he quizzed.

"I just don't know how to feel right now."

Lester pursed his lips. "I can't say as I blame you, Emily. I'm getting used to it myself," he admitted. Then, in a mock toast with an imaginary empty glass in his hand, he said "To new habits!"

The gesture struck Emily as funny coming from the life-long non-drinker.

"To new habits," she parroted. *Amen*, she thought.

Daniel was awake now and looked up at Lester with big, liquid brown eyes.

"Little man, good morning. I hoped that you would grace us with your presence," he said.

Daniel giggled at the older man's voice. Lester grinned back at him with a jack-o-lantern smile.

"Did you see that? He laughed at me!" Lester announced, dancing a modified Irish jig.

Jennie Mae watched the whole episode with smiling eyes. After her pact with Emily, she had said very little. She did give Emily a comforting wink, though.

Emily knew she could count on Jennie Mae. For the moment, she had side-stepped a minefield. She was confident they could pull off their plan. Emily had no misgivings about slipping Jennie Mae a guide showing the locations of Lester's twin hiding places.

"I am a Christian woman; I gave you my word," she told Emily.

"I will let you know if I need a favor from you. For now, my job is to take care of Mr. Taylor."

"I've never seen him so happy. Ever."

Jennie Mae turned serious. "It took a long time. He was badly addicted, Emily. Morphine almost killed him. I've seen many good men go that way, just sleeping their lives away."

Neither felt the need to discuss the inheritance money. Emily was happy that Jennie Mae had been included in Lester's will.

Imagine that, Emily thought, watching him play with her son. *Lester laughing and dancing.*

The conductor blew on his whistle. "All Aboard!"

Emily hugged her uncle one more time. He boarded the train and found his seat. His posture was rigid as if staving off more feelings. He plopped down and stared out the window. The train made a loud noise, rolled backwards and started its momentum. Emily smiled and waved, bouncing Daniel up and down. Lester wiped his eyes, held his hand up and twiddled his fingers. In less than a minute, the train slipped over the last ridge and out of view.

******

The Texas Rangers rose early that morning and shoveled their belongings into their bags. The tangled case was almost solved and they would be heading to Austin, perhaps by nightfall.

Souther's Restaurant never failed to provide a much needed breakfast. A new menu item popped off the page. They'd never tried juice from an orange in a glass filled with ice cubes. It was like drinking the chilled and sweet nectar of the gods, especially in sand-parched Wahoo.

Louis Tillman was sparkling with energy as he chomped away at his food. The lieutenant's demeanor was the opposite. He felt it coming on: it was a mixture of feelings that seemed to hit this point in an investigation. Nevertheless, he settled on the idea of knowing this whole thing was almost over.

Soon he would be writing the final report with Tillman's help, talking to the attorneys about the outcome and going through the monkey show of a trial. The trial was one thing about the system he hated. At least Texas had no barriers to executing murderers. It had a long history of those dating back to Sam Houston's days.

He despised the long days in court listening to the attorneys drone on when he would rather be in the field with Tillman solving crimes.

One thing Cramer really enjoyed was the final confrontation when all the evidence was on the table. He would spend most of the remaining time trying to determine what the perpetrator's reaction would be.

Sometimes they would protest their innocence. Other times they'd cry and tell all in a plea for forgiveness. Cramer watched helplessly as one sorrowful criminal slipped past unwary officers and shot himself in his dressing room after Tillman had spent hours playing carpenter with the man's excuses and lies.

"Have our notes been delivered, Louis?"

Tillman nodded and looked up between more helpings eggs and chorizo.

"The actors will be on the stage at 3 o'clock," *lootenant.*"

"I'll wire Austin and have another Ranger get own here and keep an eye on things," Cramer said. He pushed his chair back, left the table and returned with a fresh cup of coffee. He sat back sipping the sweet coffee and swore never to drink Chicory coffee again.

Cramer wondered why his sergeant had such a huge appetite this morning. "So, Louis...you know, it's time for The Game," Cramer said. This was a cue to play the usual round of "The End

152

Game." When the two had arrived at an appropriate place in the case, they would privately scribble their chief suspect's name on paper and compare the results later.

No reason had to be given, just a name. Pulling out their pens, they would scrawl on a napkin or any available paper and make the exchange. Afterwards, the lawmen would talk about their conclusions. Neither could remember when there hadn't been a match.

Tillman stopped eating, swallowed a bite of chorizo and looked up, surprised. "Now, sir? Can't I finish breakfast?"

Cramer cracked a smile at his partner's enthusiasm. "Okay, *after* we eat, Sergeant. I wouldn't want to be responsible for the consequences of dragging you away from that table."

"Yes sir. I guess *we* know who's going to be in jail tonight. The fun part will begin when *they* find out."

******

Willie Green stared at his Texas Ranger "invitation" in absolute terror. *This is it,* he thought. *Do I stay and face the police or get some money and run?*

If he failed to show at the jail, he'd be lucky to get out of the county, much less the huge sprawl of Texas before another taciturn Texas Ranger would hunt him down.

Panicking now, he couldn't think straight. Willie heard the tales about Texas Rangers who sported a "shoot first, ask questions later policy." Not all of them were stories, either.

He considered his choices. If he stayed, his father might be angry at first, but he'd probably throw any amount of money at the problem. If he left, the spigot would be closed, probably forever.

Better to face the wrath of his father; he would force himself to keep his mouth shut until after the old man had spewed his nasty

153

venom. It worked before and Willie thought there'd be no reason it wouldn't work again.

He racked his brain thinking about the contents of his letters to Daniels. They couldn't be used against him, he hadn't written anything incriminating, at least that he could remember.

Maybe this was a bluff by the detectives and another reason to show up and refute their evidence. He had to see what they had and what they didn't. At the very least, he knew his father would bail him out of jail if he was arrested and then he could disappear, if things were that bad.

Willie made his decision. He would defend himself with his father by his side. His plan to stay had better work or he'd wind up in every lawyer's nastiest nightmare–a Texas prison.

*****

CHAPTER TWENTY FOUR:
AN INVITING ACCUSATION

Regis Green knew about the Texas Ranger's invitations to Welborn, Manstill and his son Willie, but he wasn't invited. For once, he was powerless to influence events in Wahoo and he didn't like it at all. He paced his office and looked for the thousandth time at the mahogany grandfather clock: 2:30.

He knew Lieutenant Cramer already called his home office in Austin earlier that day and requested another deputy be sent to Wahoo; his driver Raymond overheard the telephone call in the administrative office and told Regis immediately.

If there was a good thing about this turn of events, it was the fact he was *not* invited to the jail; that would mean Regis was a suspect. He gauged the rangers would come to him when their meeting ended; they would detail their investigation and announce any arrests. For many reasons, he wasn't looking forward to it.

******

Sheriff Red Woodward sat in his small, cramped office in the jail and waited stoically for the meeting to start. He knew the two Rangers must have some evidence against someone to call this meeting in the first place; the question was, who did they think killed Hamilton Daniels and how much evidence did they have?

He opened his right drawer and looked at Daniels' letters he had liberated from Daniels' friend. No one else had these letters, so he doubted the meeting was about them. He knew without the letters, the lawmen had nothing.

No, the Rangers were coming to his jail for another reason. He removed his gun from his holster and checked it. If the Lone Star

State lawmen were coming for him he would surprise them, because Sheriff Red Woodward was going to go down fighting if it came down to that.

******

Frank Manstill checked his watch, took one last look at his ranch and rode in a quick gallop to Wahoo.

******

"It's about time, Louis."

The sergeant rose from his chair, gathered some notes and joined his boss as they walked deliberately to the jail in the heavy heat. Both men noticed the stares from some of the town folk as they strode north. No one spoke to them as they walked. The entire dusty town seemed to be holding its breath.

A hundred yards away from the jail, they were startled as Frank Manstill rode wordlessly by them on his horse; Cramer had his right hand on his gun at the sound of the horse coming up behind them; for a second, he felt like he was back in France and walking toward the Germans and their damned machine gun nests.

Except now there were no Germans staring at them, just curious Texans, he realized. He wiped the sweat on his forehead away with a small handkerchief and continued walking with Tillman slightly to the left and behind him.

Tillman ignored the gawking citizens and kept his eyes forward and locked on the jail. He glanced at the lieutenant, who kept looking around as he walked. "It's alright, sir. We're almost out of here," he said softly.

If Cramer heard, he did not acknowledge Tillman's words. He was too busy forgetting a bad memory and concentrating on his task.

"When is our relief due here?" Tillman asked, louder this time.

"In three hours," Cramer tersely answered. "We'll be heading

156

back on the five o'clock overnighter to Austin."

"Good. I'm getting rather tired of our accommodations at the Ram's Inn, myself, *lootenant*."

Cramer laughed out loud at Tillman's joke. "Someone's going to be staying here tonight – I'm sure they'd take the Ram's Inn over this," Cramer answered as they approached the one-story, L-shaped jail.

Next to the jailhouse door, Town Deputy Don Peterson sat in his customary slumped manner. Like their last visit, he didn't get up as the two Texas Rangers approached.

"You might want to get up this time," Tillman growled at the lackadaisical deputy when they were ten feet away.

Startled out of his sleepy cocoon, the deputy stood and if it were possible, assumed a position of semi-attention. Sergeant Tillman sometimes had that effect on people.

"Keep a sharp eye out, Deputy Peterson," Cramer added half-sarcastically as he opened the door and stepped inside with Louis a step behind, still glowering at the deputy.

All the invitees were there: Frank Manstill, Willie Green, Jack Welborn and Sheriff Red Woodward. There were two chairs arranged in the middle of the room ringed by four others at every major compass point. Cramer looked at the arrangement, shrugged and sat down, followed by Louis.

The two officers sat in the middle and arranged their papers. Neither spoke for a moment as the tension skyrocketed in the small room.

Willie Green could not stand the silence. "So, why are we here, officers?"

Cramer smiled and glanced at Louis. "I knew the lawyer would talk first. They always do."

"Yes, sir." Tillman seemed to enjoy this repartee.

"Please dispense with the jokes, gentlemen," Willie sneered.

Cramer fixed the lawyer with his best 'evil eye.' "Okay, counselor. Here's what we know." He outlined the basic facts of Hamilton's death – method of death and approximate time of death in a clinical flatness in his voice. "We know he was attacked but he didn't die at once; someone came by and killed him as he lay in the quarry badly wounded."

As the lieutenant spoke, Louis inspected each of the four suspects: Green fidgeted in his chair, Woodward stared at the lieutenant and Manstill looked bored. Welborn had his eyes partially closed but was shaking slightly.

"Now we get to the good part," Cramer said. "How Daniels died, we now know with an absolute certainty." He paused. "Now we find out why, and by whom. Sergeant Tillman," Cramer said, deferring to his deputy. "Please explain what I mean."

"Gladly, sir. It doesn't stop there, though. We have three dead men: Hamilton Daniels, Bubba Crosbie, and Frank Gambone. What do they all have in common? Two worked at Manstill's Ranch and the other at the Brickhouse. Two of them were in a fight in a bar. I say there are too many connections here to be a coincidence."

He continued, "Here's what we think happened: Daniels and Gambone got into a fight. However, Daniels did not die that night. We know that because of a restaurant receipt dated the next afternoon, as the lieutenant just said. No, he was killed when Frank Gambone was already out of town on the cattle drive. That's a fact."

At the mention of the restaurant receipt proving Daniels died the next evening, all their heads snapped almost as one towards him.

"So Gambone didn't kill Daniels?" Green asked incredulously.

"No. He couldn't have killed Daniels, even though he wanted to.

158

We also know that because someone also tried to make it look like Daniels died that night of the brawl, thereby pointing the finger at Gambone."

"How do you know that?" Welborn asked.

"Simple. When we found Daniel's body, he had already been in the Icehouse and then placed *back* at the murder scene shortly before we got here. The Texas sun took care of the rest," Cramer said. "But we found secondary burned skin because of the body being frozen shortly after death and then thawed out, then re-frozen."

"The human skin is not that much different than hamburger, actually," Louis added professorially. "This process left unique marks on the body which we found the second time we saw Daniel's body."

Cramer said, "When we first saw the body in the Icehouse; there were broken arteries in the neck and hands that we saw. That explains the red splotches," Cramer added. "They were obviously there the second time we examined the body. By then they had set in. Also, the wounds inflicted showed he was attacked twice."

"Correct, sir. Then we looked at the photos and saw the restaurant receipt. The mayor's photographer was good. He was almost too good, actually. But no such receipt was given to us – by anyone." Louis Tillman stared at Sheriff Woodward, who knew enough to keep his mouth shut.

"Then it was a process of elimination. Gambone was probably murdered and made to look like an accident; unless someone confesses to that killing, we can't prove it. But it is logical. When evidence showed that Gambone was gone the time Daniels was murdered, he was no longer useful as a scapegoat," Cramer said with an eye on Frank Manstill.

"No, the real question is… who would want Hamilton Daniels dead?"

No one spoke. The suspects all did. It was Lieutenant Cramer who dropped the big truth bomb. "Then we got some letters from Daniels' friend Hayden. And it all came together." Both Woodward and Green stared open-mouthed at the officer.

"Interesting things in here, Willie," Tillman idly remarked. "It was easy when we figured out who 'U U' was. It meant 'W.' Which means you, Mr. Green," he parried.

"Daniels knew you were coming back to Wahoo. We know he was involved in a previous attempt to blackmail your father because of you. Hayden told us that. So he was killed before you got here. And it was probably on your orders he was killed. We'll prove that later in court."

Green was stunned, but managed an answer. "You'll never prove that," he croaked.

"Oh, I'm sure someone here will fill us in on the details," Cramer replied. "Eventually." He fingered his cane.

"We also know you, Jack, were there at least twice – once when Daniels was murdered, and later when his body was moved. We'll prove that later in court, as well," Tillman said.

"Last but not least, we have the Sheriff here who hid the letters from us and stole the receipt from the body. Any reason for that, Red?"

"To Hell with you," he spat towards Cramer, who ignored it.

"What about Crosbie?" That's the third one," Green asked.

"Sergeant Tillman Louis got him with a perfect shot in town. Crosbie died riding away from town but someone took his weapons. He was heading towards north, probably to your ranch, Frank. After all, he wore your colors."

Manstill shrugged. "A lot of men have."

"Perhaps," Tillman answered. "So, here's what we think what did

160

happen: Daniels was in a fight with Gambone and then lured to the site at the quarry. There he was attacked with a knife and stabbed at least four times. But he wasn't dead. Jack Welborn came back later and finished the job with a hammer to the head. That killed Daniels, all right.

The next day Roger Deacon found the body. He ran into Welborn's office and told him there had been an accident. Welborn called Regis Green and said there was a dead body. He couldn't have known that unless he had already known about the murder."

Welborn openly sighed at this fact.

"So we asked ourselves, who would have the most to lose if Daniels were alive? And the answer is you, Willie. You knew if there were another scandal your father would disinherit you, so you arranged to have Daniels killed before you arrived. It almost worked."

Willie Green trembled at this accusation. *What else did they have?*

"Here is the final piece of the puzzle: the photos were snapped and the body was taken to the Icehouse. Then it was moved back outside to appear he died later. That was a mistake. Had the body remained in the Icehouse, we wouldn't have figured that out."

The sunlight shining through the Jail House windows revealed the dust dancing in the torpid air. The accused men slumped in their chairs and looked down at the wooden floor as the last piece of the Wahoo Murder Puzzle played out.

"So," Tillman continued, "We have the letters implicating Willie Green, Jack Welborn either doing the killing originally or at least coming back to finish the job later and the sheriff holding back evidence and impeding our investigation, although I think the sheriff also participated in killing Daniels somehow. "

The guilty silence of the accused men hung in the stifling air of the jail.

A moment later, the two lawmen looked at each other as if by prearranged signal.

"*Lootenant*, will you do the honors?" Tillman asked, wanting to get this over as soon as possible. He kept both eyes on Sheriff Woodward.

Cramer stood and unfastened his pistol methodically as he spoke. Tillman also stood, weapon in hand and aimed at Woodward and Welborn's direction. Only the sheriff was armed.

"William Harden Green, you are charged and under arrest with murder and conspiracy in the death of Hamilton Daniels; Jack Welborn, you are also under arrest for the same charges; Sheriff Woodward, you are also under arrest and immediate suspension as a Texas Officer of the Peace for concealing evidence and conspiracy. We'll work on murder charges later."

Both Green and Welborn blanched a deep pale hue as Cramer made this announcement; Woodward slowly reached for his gun at his side.

"Don't do it, Sheriff, Tillman warned. "I have the drop on you and I *will* shoot. "It's over, Red."

Woodward stopped still and realized his position was hopeless. "You're right. You got me on the draw." He held up both hands and stood up.

Tillman disarmed Woodward and handcuffed him while Cramer handcuffed Willie Green and Jack Welborn. All three men were then cuffed together in a method called the "Ranger Rope," which was a long chain looped through the handcuffs behind the suspect's backs; it only allowed a foot or so of movement in any direction at the same time.

"I guess I can go. You didn't say anything about *me* being arrested," Manstill cagily remarked as the men were seated roughly and without ceremony on the floor of the largest cell.

"We can always come back, but right now, we don't have enough to take you to jail, Frank." Tillman said. "You're free to go."

"We know you met with Regis Green at least once but we don't have any proof on him being involved – yet," Cramer also admonished the rancher.

"You can tell him that."

Manstill's lips tweaked into a small smile. "Maybe I will."

"Excellent. In the meantime, would you tell the deputy outside to step in here?" I have a promotion for him," Cramer said. "He's now the Sheriff."

Frank Manstill found his hat, put it on, and walked out without saying goodbye to the Rangers. A moment later, a bewildered Town Deputy Peterson appeared in the door.

"Sheriff?" he asked as he saw his boss handcuffed and sitting on the floor.

"He's not the sheriff any more. You are, Peterson. Until Texas Ranger Slim Hannibal comes and relieves you, you are in charge of the prisoners. He'll transport them to the county seat for arraignment and trial. When he gets here, you do as he says. No need to put more people in jail today, right?" Cramer said with a slight wink.

"When is the Ranger coming and why only one of them?" the dazed former deputy asked.

"He'll be here in three or four hours is the answer to your first question. Ask to your second query, he's a Texas Ranger. One is enough to do the job."

*****

CHAPTER TWENTY FIVE:
ENDINGS

Lester never noticed the deception. Upon her arrival in Oak Park, Jennie Mae deposited Emily's pilfered items in the hiding places Lester had secreted inside his study. Lester unexpectedly entered the room while she was setting fire to the only proof of Emily's misdeeds: the handwritten directions to the vaults. Jennie Mae calmly explained her actions as ridding him of some old bank documents.

Clean from morphine for good, Lester relished his last years. The miser-turned-humanitarian even bought a telephone for Emily and Roger's house in Wahoo. He called them weekly and delighted in hearing his nephew's tinny voice through the earpiece.

The Deacons accepted Lester's invitations to visit him at Oak Park. The lively family reunions with hurried preparations and presents always ended with melancholy farewells. Each visit brought a renewed friendship between Emily and Jennie Mae, though they never spoke about the money and jewels.

Lester grew fond of the Deacons, and he fought his longing for them by staying active in local politics. After a local fire burned two Oak Park houses, he tried in vain to lobby for a neighborhood fire station. The campaign was time well spent: it allowed him to meet new acquaintances whom he ogled with tales of his travels.

Lester took four significant trips: He spent a month in British Columbia in 1927. Lester fell in love with pine-strewn woods, crystal-blue sky and the haunting beauty of the bay. The second trip was his first to San Francisco, where he and Jennie Mae spent a full month at the Freemont. He loved the exotic fragrances of the city's Chinatown district and which made Lester's memories of the Far East more piquant.

A third trip to London did not go so well, as he tried to reconcile with his long-lost son, Richard, now forty-three and bloated like a traditional English pig. "Go to Hell, old man," his only son yelled at him when Lester knocked on the door of Richard's Mayfair apartment.

Finally, Lester went back to his favorite city, New York, where he auctioned a collection of his finest jewelry and artifacts at Christie's. The sale netted his estate more than $290,000. He anonymously donated a portion of the earnings to an orphanage on Chicago's South Side. He attended both games of the 1928 World Series in Yankee Stadium and through his connections, got a baseball signed by Babe Ruth.

Jennie Mae was always at his side and faithfully handled all the travel details; it made the old man's life easier, she knew. She was the most amazed at Lester's change of character among all others in Lester's tight circle of friends and relatives.

After returning from a chilly weekend hunting trip across the Canadian border in March 1929, Lester fell gravely ill with a cold that developed into pneumonia. The doctors gave him less than three days to live; he toughed it out for almost two weeks.

Jennie Mae and Emily were at his side in his mansion when he died on March 30, 1929. At his written request, he was cremated and his ashes were taken to Victoria in British Columbia where they were scattered over the bay on a sun-drenched April day.

Lester left $200,000 each to Richard Taylor, his son in Great Britain, as well as Emily and Roger. He left $100,000 to Jennie Mae. All of Lester's stocks and bonds were sold well before the Black Friday came in October 1929.

Lester wanted his mansion demolished and the property returned to the city. In its place stands today an expansive, two-story residential fire station. Before the last parts of the edifice were completed, an anonymous donor bought two new shiny-red fire engines for the new station.

The remaining $300,000 from his estate went to the Chicago Natural Art Museum. The gift included Lester's African art collection, which spurred the opening of the Lester Hopewell Taylor Wing in 1937. The Museum was partially destroyed in a 1966 fire but private donations paid for its rebuilding in 1974.

Much of Lester's collection is still there.

******

Melinda Sullivan Gunderson never married.

In 1934, she made good on her dream. She became the first University of Texas graduate to become a female doctor in the state. She joined the U.S. Army Women's Army Corps eleven years after her trip to Wahoo. She served in World War II and during the raging maelstrom of Korea.

Melinda Gunderson retired from the army as a Lieutenant Colonel and opened a private medical practice in Houston; it took a long time before the woman doctor could gain the trust of local residents. Persistence and professionalism eventually won their hearts and she accepted the adoring title of "Miz Doc" Gunderson.

She also became a noted disease specialist. In 1956, she helped discover and research a new disease involving the central nervous system, now classified as Gunderson's Syndrome.

Melinda retired to Hawaii in 1971 to write three scholastic books on disease control for the American Medical Association. She died in 1981 at the age of 78. A bust statue of Melinda Sullivan Gunderson is installed in Austin's Texas Women's Hall of Fame and stands as a memorial to her medical contributions.

******

Jellison Briscoe kept the Ram's Inn solvent but he never refurbished it. Regis Green's daughter Clarissa eventually bought

166

it for $25,000, tore it down in 1936 and built the New Wahoo Inn, a three-story, Victorian-style hotel. In 1999, the hotel burned down in an electrical fire.

Briscoe took off for Chicago, Illinois. Going into business with a cousin, he opened a small bar with a four-room brothel located in Cicero, Al Capone's home turf. Two years later, in 1938, Briscoe was accidentally shot to death while arbitrating an argument between two drunken out-of-towners over a card game.

******

Frank Manstill was never named in the official investigation of Daniels' murder. Although Tillman suspected Frank's role was greater than he let on, Louis knew there was no direct evidence to link him to the crime or even get an indictment.

The cagey rancher eventually bought an automobile and proudly drove it into town every Saturday. Unlike many other land owners, he won an important state court case in 1935 to keep his cattle land from being taken by the government for the building of a highway.

He continued running his prosperous ranch his way until his death in October 1945 from kidney failure. Manstill managed to outlive another wife, his fourth. He was 83.

Manstill's son, Alexander, was wounded at Pearl Harbor while in the Navy onboard the *Arizona*. He received a Purple Heart for his wounds which his father proudly displayed in the ranch's spacious living room.

The Manstill Cattle Ranch lasted until 1978; Alexander Manstill died of brain cancer and there were no heirs to the family business. The Texan government finally moved in and a new highway was built through the upper half of the property. At the same time, the government purchased the remaining Manstill land which became the site of a U.S. Air Force flight test facility for NASA astronauts.

Some people report seeing a strange light where the old ranch house once sat; others say it's the ghost of Frank Manstill, bemoaning the loss of his family's lost land.

******

Jennie Mae Bullock remained in Oak Park after Lester passed away. She and her husband George used part of the gift money to open a furniture store which Emily and Roger allowed to be filled with Lester's furnishings.

She also invested $30,000 in the stock market and cashed out (according to Lester's recommendation) in days before The Crash. She earned $100,000 for the risk which she stashed in the basement of her new house.

Jennie's husband George Bullock died of peritonitis in 1942. Although she had suitors, Jennie Mae never remarried.

The investment earnings and her thriving store provided financial security, even through the Depression years; her customers included those who were marginally employed as well as the many cash-strapped socialites who had also fallen on hard times; they could no longer afford their huge houses and staff and were looking for a bargain.

In 1950, she sold the store for a handsome profit and moved to Ryder, Tennessee to be near her two sisters. Always a generous woman, Jennie Mae supported her family by paying the college tuitions for her two nephews and financing a business for her second cousin.

On November 4, 1960, she died at the age of 71, surrounded by friends and family in Ryder.

*****

Wesley Oliver Holmes III left Texas forever after the Wahoo fiasco.

He returned to New York and worked for a time in newspaper

168

advertising and later in the new field of public relations for a soap company. He prospered in his new role until it went bankrupt in 1933. During the Depression, he worked as a well-paid researcher at the New York Times.

His plans to write his own book never materialized.

Holmes never stopped smoking marijuana and was arrested in 1940 for possession in a Harlem jazz club. Even his legal connections through his famous uncle failed to help and he was sentenced to a year in New York's Sing-Sing prison in Ossining, New York.

After his release in February 1941, he moved to upper New York State. When World War II started, he tried to enlist as a war correspondent but was turned down because of his marijuana possession conviction. A few months later, he got another newspaper job through another relative and was hired by the Copley News Service as an overseas reporter in Australia.

On June 1, 1942 his military plane with twenty other souls onboard left Hawaii's Henderson Field for the trip to his new job. A few hours later, the craft developed engine trouble and crashed near the island of Palmyra, 350 miles southwest of Hawaii.

There were no survivors.

******

Sheriff Red Woodward and William Harden Green went on trial for the murder of Hamilton Daniels on January 12, 1927.

Woodward's lawyer, who was paid by Regis Green, managed to place doubt in the jurors' minds about his defendant's guilt. After a six-week trial, Woodward was acquitted of murder. However, he was sentenced to three years for conspiracy to commit murder, a far lesser charge than the florid-faced prosecutor originally wanted.

Woodward served his time and then disappeared into the huge wilderness of the Great Depression.

Willie Green's fate was far different. Three days before his trial, he pled guilty to the same charge as Woodward and received a year in prison and three years probation, thanks to his father's connections in Austin.

He did not fare as well in prison, however. Three times he was beaten by other inmates and was finally moved to the state's Old Wall Prison located in Huntsville. Inside its red walls, Green helped other inmates with their legal matters and earned him the nickname "The Counselor."

Released in January 1928, he returned to Wahoo a few months before his broken-hearted father Regis Green died of a heart attack in May, exactly two years to the day Hamilton Daniels was murdered.

Freed of his father's wishes, Willie sold the factory to an Eastern company and fled to Europe, where he lived in Paris and London. His sister took over the hotel and other family interests in town. Willie didn't care. He cashed the checks and gallivanted around Europe.

He almost squandered his fortune in Paris after being exploited by the raw and decadent homosexual world surrounding him. He awoke, still drunk from the night before, in a grimy Paris garret in late 1932 and decided to try something different by going straight, at least on the surface.

Willie Green arrived in London and within two months was introduced to a rich widow who fell in love with him, past and all. A former beauty queen, Rosalind Merton-Green agreed to take care of Willie if he would be her personal social escort. Indeed, she would tolerate his eccentric dalliances, she said, as long as he was discreet. He was, and the couple lived the high life through America's Depression in the 1930's. For Willie, it was the best of both worlds.

On August 21, 1940, the London society scion from Wahoo, Texas was killed instantly when a five-hundred-pound bomb from a Luftwaffe bomber narrowly missed the Grimy Goose, a pub Willie frequented, but instead smashed his small downtown residence into dust during the Battle of Britain.

For more than a year, Rosalind pined for her lost Willie. She eventually skipped down the altar with a man from Surrey who had captivated her, primarily with his title of Baron. He was actually little more than a commoner who bought a title with stolen money; he ultimately swindled Rosalind out of her entire fortune in a phony oil drilling scheme in Greenland in 1951.

******

Jack Welborn was granted immunity from prosecution and at Cramer's urging was ready to testify against Woodward. But with the plea bargains of Green and Woodward, the trial never happened. He left town, though -- he moved to Missouri, where he worked as a foreman in a rock quarry near St. Louis.

On March 31, 1932, he was crushed to death with two other men when a crane holding two tons of stone collapse in Enid, Oklahoma. The death was ruled an accident because of the faulty welds discovered in the crane's structure.

*****

Roger and Emily Deacon stayed in Wahoo. Roger did not have to testify at Sheriff Woodward's trial and for many years afterward refused to talk to anyone about the murder. Emily could always tell when he was thinking about it, though.

Despite Doc Manley's opinion, they never had any more children after Daniel. It didn't matter because Daniel and his wife Linda gave the Deacon's five grandchildren, which blessed Roger and Emily in their elder years.

After Willie Green sold the Brick Factory, Roger stayed under the new owners and promoted to General Manager in 1940, a position he held until the factory closed its doors for good in late 1953. The domestic market for toughened red bricks gave way to cheaper, lighter housing materials in the boom years after World

War II.

He and Emily then moved to a two-story house in the small, blossoming burg of Renton in Washington State. Roger opened his own construction company with son Daniel and for ten years his business boomed as the neighboring cities of Seattle, Tacoma and Puyallup grew to almost a million people.

In 1964 he sold the business, leased out his Renton home and bought an eight-room, large Victorian-style rambler house in North Tacoma. Tucked along a lush knoll overlooking Commencement Bay, Roger lived in this the sprawling house peacefully until his death by a heart attack on October 18, 1971. He was 73.

Emily took Lester's advice and stayed away from the stock market. Instead, she bought gold and silver which served as collateral for Roger's business. Lester's generous inheritance also helped pay for their lovely Tacoma house. Around Tacoma for those in the know, it was no secret that Emily Deacon was the financial whiz behind her husband's success.

She corresponded regularly with Jennie Mae Bullock, and after witnessing discrimination of her friend, she donated money to civil rights causes in the 1960's.

Ten years after Roger died, Emily passed away at the age of 80. She left her fortune of $1.4 million to her beloved grandchildren. Emily made arrangements for the eight-room mansion to be donated to the local town. A two-year renovation followed; it is now a popular public library and museum.

******

Daniel Hawthorne Deacon graduated with a Degree in Engineering in 1947. In 1951, he was drafted into the US Army and promoted to Major in the US Army Engineering Corps. He stayed in that war-torn country until his discharge in 1953. While he was in the Army, a scruffy clerk noticed the Major's birthplace and remarked about it; Major Dan Deacon then became "Wahoo Dan" to is troops and is a nickname he still has to this day.

*****

Today, Wahoo is uninhabited but for about two dozen old-timers and a handful of Mexican immigrants on their way to other parts.

Most of the old buildings were torn down—or fell down on their own—in the late seventies. The destruction created large scattered spaces along the horizon that gave the town a gap-toothed appearance. It still has a post office and a gas station. A convenience store took over the building that housed the legendary Souther's Restaurant, renowned for its fine food and delicious coffee.

Fifty years after the closing of the Brick House, any visitor would find himself facing a ghost of a town with boarded-up windows and a stir of tumbleweeds.

When Frank Manstill's son sold his father's land, only the nearby Air Force base was left. The officers and civilians only come into town long enough to gas their cars. As far as any outsider could tell, Wahoo was dead. No one cared to hear the story about who killed Hamilton Daniels or why.

*****

EPILOGUE

Louis Tillman retired as a *Lootenant* after all. In 1929, he finally received the coveted gold bar and the command of a prestigious district in Dallas. After solving various other cases and opening dozens more, he retired as a virtual criminologist legend in 1934 after serving as a Texas Ranger for 32 years.

He moved again, this time to San Francisco, where he bought a small houseboat he named *The Wahoo* in the city's Marina District. He continued dabbling in crime-solving as a paid consultant for the San Francisco Police Department and was a major contributor to solving the infamous Chinatown murders in 1943.

Louis Tillman never saw Lucille Fay LeSueur again after their meeting in Texas so long ago.

Louis lived on *The Wahoo* on his $474 monthly pension and even found love at last, marrying his devoted wife, Donna Maranville, in 1935. Their first date was at a movie: In October 1934 they saw *Chained,* starring Joan Crawford and Clark Gable.

He was a doting father to his half-daughter, Cora and an even better grandfather to her two children. Donna and Louis lived together contently for fifteen years before he died on his birthday on December 2, 1949. He was 70.

Donna sold the boat and moved back to her home roots in Katy, Texas. Asking nothing more out of life than being buried next to her beloved Louis, she had his coffin exhumed and buried again in Memorial Cemetery south of Dallas. Every Sunday around noon she went to his grave, plucked away the stray weeds and laid a fresh wreath on it.

Donna Marie Tillman was buried alongside Louis after she followed him in death a little more than nine years to the day he died. On January 2, 1958 she breathed her last and died in her daughter Cora's arms at 73.

On his gravestone she had *Louis Tillman, Texas Ranger* engraved on the pale red marble surface. Beneath his name was a replica of his old Texas Ranger shield and his old badge number, 751. The Rangers retired his number out of respect. Below the shield, which was outlined in gold, were words that sum up the entire story: *Case Closed.*

******

Marcus T. Cramer stayed in the Texas Rangers for ten more years before he was medically retired in 1937 as a high-level Captain. The knee he wounded in Wahoo plagued him for years afterwards and eventually became arthritic. Two surgeries failed to fix it. His cane became as much a part of him as his good leg and he used it well when dealing with criminals.

The lawman became a roving inspector for the Texas Rangers and saw his former partner fairly often. After Prohibition ended, he even defied his dead Irish mother and sat in many a bar while Louis, drinking sparingly as usual, reminisced with him about old times. But Marcus was content to sip a coffee in those forays with Louis. Just being with the old friend was almost enough to make him forget the pain in his knee from so long ago.

He stayed in touch with Louis and even became his best man when he married Donna. Three times a year he ventured out to San Francisco and rode on Louis' boat and enjoyed the company of his friend, who actually turned out to be a pretty good boat captain for a Texas boy.

On November 3, 1949, Marcus got a telephone call from Donna. Louis was very sick with a bad case of pneumonia. Marcus immediately left his home near Dallas and boarded his first airplane and flew to San Francisco to see his stricken friend. Louis briefly rallied against the illness for almost a month after Marcus arrived. But his lungs were just too full of fluid and the doctors did everything they could to save him.

With Donna at his side and a grieving Marcus crying silently in the hospital room's corner, Louis Tillman looked at her for one last time, closed his eyes and said, "At least I am not going out the same way I came in: broke, naked and searching for something."

Marcus did everything he could to console Donna but he had no one to console him.

His own wife, Renee Cramer (nee Granger), whom he married in 1932, died in a freak hunting accident on September 1, 1946. She and Marcus were grouse hunting near Dallas when her shotgun misfired and exploded. It was later determined some loose dirt jammed the firing chamber, causing the firing pin to malfunction and explode. It killed her instantly. Louis immediately flew to help his friend through the funeral and the subsequent days. Marcus grieved for two weeks on the *Wahoo* as Louis' guest until he emerged from the extra berth room a completely changed man.

After Renee died, Marcus lived alone quietly, occasionally teaching Criminology classes at The University of Texas. He tried his hand at writing and even completed a book shortly before his death; a compilation of cases he and Louis worked on back in the "good old days." The book was never published in his lifetime.

Marcus T. Cramer, retired Texas Ranger Captain, died on July 16, 1970, in Austin of heart failure. He was 75.

In 1974, his sister Lorena Cramer May, found the half-mildewed manuscript in her attic during a routine spring cleaning. She submitted it to a publisher who eagerly proceeded to steal most of the profits from "Great Texas Ranger Mysteries" by Captain Marcus T. Cramer, Texas Ranger.

Over thirty-five thousand copies were sold before being relegated to musty non-fiction sections of the nation's public and school libraries.

The Wahoo triple slayings are never mentioned.

*****

Changing her name to Joan Crawford, she left Louis' life and went on to star in movies for almost 22 years as a leading lady at Metro-Goldwyn-Mayer Studio Hollywood. After successive films lost money, she was labeled "Box Office Poison" and famously dropped from her contract in 1944.

Joan showed the industry it was wrong by winning three Best Actress nominations in 1945, 1947 and 1952. Her Oscar win capped her "comeback" Oscar in 1945 in a memorable role as a business owner in "Mildred Pierce." She was a dominant Hollywood figure for almost 45 years before she was through.

However, most moviegoers remember her better in her role opposite Bette Davis in 1962 in "Whatever Happened to Baby Jane?"

"Sure, I wanted to be famous, just to make the kids who'd laughed at me feel foolish. I wanted to be rich, so I'd never have to do the awful work my mother did and live at the bottom of the barrel – ever. And I wanted to be a dancer because I loved to dance. I always knew, whether I was in school or working in some damned dime-store, that I'd make it," she remembered for an interviewer in three years before her death in Los Angeles.

A year after Joan's death in 1977 at 72, her daughter Christine Crawford wrote a "tell-all" book about their difficult relationship. "Mommie Dearest" became a box-office smash hit and ultimately was a socially-conscious cult movie favorite as well. Joan Crawford's reputation took a major public nosedive with her sudden exposure in the movie as a sodden alcoholic, perhaps even a borderline manic-depressive and a notoriously abusive mother.

Nevertheless, in 2001, she was voted one of the "Top Ten Actresses in the 20th century" by the Academy of Arts and Letters.

In 1963, Joan hired a private detective to find out whatever happened to Louis Tillman. When she got the answer in a large manila folder a few weeks later, she cried for a day at what could have been, dropped the papers into the fireplace and burned them.

THE END

ABOUT THE AUTHOR

The son of a career Navy carrier pilot, Gerald A. Loeb served in the US Army as an enlisted soldier in the late 1970s and was commissioned as a Second Lieutenant in 1983. He served in Saudi Arabia as a US Army Reserve Captain in the Operation Desert Storm/Enduring Freedom.

In May 1983, he was graduated from San Jose State University with a B.A. of Communications in Journalism with Minors in Military Science and World History. He has written in various newspapers and periodicals in the US as well as Europe, where he resided for 15 years.

Gerald has toiled in distinctly different jobs: journalist, soldier, collections agent, English teacher, cemetery worker, paperboy, busboy and general administrative drone jobs with a short stint in car sales.

His other fiction novels include "No More Moves" (1993), and "The Perfect Glitch" (2018). "Politically Derelict" (2016) and "Politically Derelict, Vol. 2" (2018) are a series of satirical political humor.

Mr. Loeb currently resides in sunny Albuquerque, New Mexico where he cheers on his beloved New York Yankees. He is currently working on his next novel, "The Stiletto Vote" (2019) and a collection of short stories about New Mexico titled "Orange Sun" (2020).

You can find his daily musings on Facebook at Jerry Loeb and Gerald A. Loeb, author, on Twitter as @geraldloeb and on Instagram at jerryloeb.

Made in the USA
Columbia, SC
04 July 2018